JET SCREAMER
ADVENTURES IN ABSURDITY

JET SCREAMER

ADVENTURES IN ABSURDITY

M. P. MACDOUGALL

ISBN: 978-1-962138-12-3

Cover design by M.P. MacDougall

This story is dedicated to my family.

Without them, I'd have very little to write about.

1

'PICNICKER' AND OTHER INSULTS

THE ENGLISH LANGUAGE IS A WONDERFULLY COMPLEX THING. IT ALLOWS single words to have wide varieties of definitions, some of them known to only a few fortunate people. The term "inside joke" is a perfect example of this. An inside joke is when a small group of people have redefined an otherwise humorless word or phrase, associating it with something hilarious. Its very name refers to the fact that the people the joke is on are on the outside, and therefore have no understanding of what is so funny.

When someone tells you, "Oh, it's an inside joke," you can bet that it's on you. I involuntarily check my fly and wipe my face every time I hear someone laughing and talking about inside jokes. Not that I'm in the habit of making myself the target of others' mirth, but one can never be too careful.

In order to avoid being on the receiving end of unnecessary ribbing, I arm myself with enough inside jokes to even things out. To that end, I've come up with my own personal definitions of many words and phrases that Mr. Webster would likely disagree with. Personally, I've always felt his work could stand a little revision, anyway.

For example, most people would tell you that a picnicker is someone who carries a meal outdoors with the intention of performing a picnic. I disagree. To me, a picnicker is any of about a thousand different types of outdoor neophytes, ranging from people who think that camping is anyplace they can park their forty foot travel trailer to those who think that if a four lane highway doesn't go there, it doesn't exist.

'Picnicker' as defined in Webster's is a seemingly innocuous term, bordering on the complimentary. It says a picnicker is "one who goes on or participates in a picnic". 'Picnic' is defined as:

- **1.** An open air meal, especially one eaten on an excursion.

- **2.** An easy task or pleasant experience.

I expand on the second explanation to get my own definition of 'picnickers'.

Put simply, picnickers are sissies.

Anybody who wants their outdoor experience to be "easy or pleasant" is a sissy in my book. I'm willing to bet that Lewis and Clark didn't invite any picnickers along when they went off in search of the Northwest Passage. Deviled eggs just don't last that long, anyway. When their food ran out along the way and they found themselves trying to come up with interesting ways to prepare dog, they may well have wished they had some deviled eggs along, but that can be excused due to the severity of their situation.

A note about deviled eggs: They are the preferred treat of most picnickers. Eating and enjoying them does not automatically make one a picnicker, but caution should be exercised around them. Caution should also be exercised around anyone who has eaten them within the last half hour, as the after effects can be quite annoying. If you go on a camping trip into a wilderness and your tent mate produces and begins to consume a supply of deviled eggs, you should first become suspicious of his character as an outdoorsman, and immediately after that, make provisions for him to sleep not only outside the tent, but ideally someplace well downwind.

The only proper place to consume deviled eggs is at large holiday feasts such as Christmas or Thanksgiving. The large quantities of other food available at these events tend to keep people from ingesting lethal doses of deviled eggs. I must admit that I have been known to be fond of the things, to the extent of throwing elbows at any of my brothers who get near the egg plate before I do. This is, of course, perfectly acceptable behavior. High society types would no doubt be appalled by such a display, but then they would probably see nothing wrong with being identified as picnickers, either.

Back to the subject at hand. Being the youngest of twelve children, I spent the better part of my life as the object of inside jokes. Being younger and less experienced, I was a likely (and easy) target. In an ideal world, siblings would treat each other with love and consideration, but my world was less than ideal. The upside of my cruel upbringing is that I got to study at the feet of masters.

My brothers and sisters (and at times, my parents) were all experts at the art of the inside joke. They'd all be laughing uproariously, and I'd be walking away thinking, "I don't get it." As I grew older and learned that many words had hidden meanings known only to my family, I started to understand what was so funny. Of course, the moment they realized I was on to them, they went off in search of other victims for their inside jokes. Now that my sense of humor was in concert with theirs, I started to realize what a fun crowd my family really was. Up to about my thirteenth birthday, I just thought they were a bunch of big meanies.

My brothers and I now have an entire vocabulary all our own, and we entertain ourselves with it on a regular basis. Almost no one outside our family understands our vocabulary or our sense of humor, and now I quite often notice people walking away from us muttering, "I don't get it" as my brothers and I hold our sides and wipe tears of hysteria from our cheeks. In order to understand our sense of humor, one must first understand our version of the English language. To that end, I've compiled a basic dictionary of terms to allow the reader near, if not inside, our inner circle of humor.

M. P. MACDOUGALL

Air Mattress - Full-body pillow for *Sissies*. Real men sleep in the dirt.

Ammunition - Too heavy to carry *Camping*. You won't need it anyway, because when your *Two Man Tent* is stomped flat by *The Foot*, you won't be able to find your *Firearm*.

Apple - A nearly round fruit that grows on trees. Ideally suited for throwing at *Dogs*, neighbor kids, passing pedestrians, and *Brothers*. When ripe, they are edible for people. When rotten, they are edible for cows. To determine ripeness, one finds a suitable target, i.e., *Dogs*, neighbor kids, *Brothers*, cows, etc. If the apple bounces off the target, it is ripe. If, upon impact, the apple resembles applesauce, it is rotten.

Axe - A club with a blunt metal end employed for breaking up firewood.

Baby Wipes - Luxury *Hygiene Item*. If *Deviled Eggs* are in play, these things aren't just for baby any more.

Backpacker - Masochist who walks into wilderness areas for his *Camping* trips, rather than driving to a developed campground.

Beer - Luxury drink too heavy to carry *Camping*. Unless you leave the *Soap* at home. Cheers!

Big Meany - Anyone who enjoys inside jokes at my expense.

• • •

BIKE HELMET - 'SAFETY' DEVICE ONLY WORN BY *GRANOLAS* AND *Politicians* to provide a false sense of security. Failure to use on your kids provides *Granolas* and *Politicians* with a false sense of superiority.

BROTHER - TORMENTOR, NEMESIS, ENEMY, *CAMPING* PARTNER, INSTIGATOR, *Big Meany*, best friend. Any of these can and do apply, depending on the situation at hand.

BUG SPRAY - SEE *LANTERN*.

CAMERA - USED FOR TAKING PHOTOS OF *BROTHERS* IN EMBARRASSING situations. *Skinny Dipping* comes to mind.

CAMPING - SELF INFLICTED OUTDOOR TORTURE. ALMOST ALWAYS FUN, IF only in retrospect.

CAMP STOVE - JET ENGINE WITHOUT THE JET ATTACHED. USED FOR JUMP starting cursing contests or igniting forest fires. Never used for heating food.

CAT - HOUSEHOLD PETS TOO SMART TO GO *CAMPING*. INSTEAD, THEY watch the house while you're gone. They sleep on the kitchen table and eat mice in the bathtub too, but hey - at least somebody's watching your house.

CELL PHONE - ELECTRONIC HANDCUFF. ONE OF THE REASONS GOD invented *Camping*.

· · ·

CHEESE - ANTIDOTE FOR *DEVILED EGGS*.

CHISEL - A TOOL USED TO DRIVE SCREWS.

CHONIES - UNFLATTERING UNDERWEAR. SEE: *TIGHTY-WHITIES*.

CLOD - SHORT FOR *CLODHOPPER*. AN UNUSUALLY DENSE PERSON. ALSO, A hard-packed ball of dirt mixed with rocks which is a great substitute for an *Apple*. Not for eating, you *Clod* - for throwing! Get it?

CLODHOPPER - CLUMSY SHOES. USUALLY WORN BY *CLODS*.

COFFEE - THE ELIXIR OF LIFE. MANY *CAMPING* TRIPS ARE CALLED OFF when it is discovered that some *Clod* forgot the *Coffee*. The *Clod* in question is sometimes required to perform a forced *Day Hike* back to the truck, so he can drive into town to bring back *Coffee*.

CRYBABY - ANYONE WHO BACKS OUT OF A *CAMPING* TRIP FOR ANY REASON. See *Picnicker*.

DAY HIKE - DEATH MARCH.

DEODORANT - MYTHICAL *HYGIENE ITEM*. TRUST ME, WE CAN STILL smell you.

DEVILED EGGS - TOXIC WASTE TOPPED WITH PAPRIKA. EDIBLE ONLY ON holidays, unless you're a *Picnicker*.

. . .

Dip - Refreshing swim. Also, a term used to describe *Skinny Dippers*.

Dog - Household pets too dumb to avoid *Camping*. Most *Dogs* actually enjoy it, since campgrounds have so many exciting options for stealing food and rolling in dead things.

Dog Dish - Any dish the *Dog* can reach.

Dog Food - Any food on or near the *Dog Dish*. Also anything the *Cat* refuses to eat.

Doof - Derived from Doofus, meaning anyone of limited or non-existent intelligence.

Dry Land Drowning - *Camping* on low ground at high tide.

Duck Hunting - Sitting in a marsh, drinking *Coffee*, and swearing at the *Dog*. Ducks seldom participate.

Ear Plugs - What the kids need while Daddy loads the truck. What Mommy wears when Daddy can't find the *Coffee*. Or the *Beer*.

Elk Hunting - Wandering aimlessly through the woods, splitting time looking for elk and the last place you saw the truck. Elk almost never participate.

. . .

FLASHLIGHT - A STORAGE CONTAINER FOR DEAD BATTERIES.

FIREARM - WHAT YOU HAVE AFTER YOU TRY TO LIGHT THE *CAMP STOVE*. Also, what you can never find in your *Two Man Tent* when *The Foot* comes knocking and you're wearing nothing but your favorite *Chonies*. Run!

GARBAGE BAG - SEE *RAIN GEAR*. ALSO USED FOR COLLECTIVELY CARRYING duck decoys far enough from the truck to make it impossible to carry them all back individually when the bag blows out.

GRANOLA - BREAKFAST FOOD CONSISTING OF SUGAR WITH A FEW DRIED oats, nuts and raisins thrown in. Also a derogatory term for anyone wearing Birkenstocks, berets, or any other remotely French fashion item. If that's too confusing, just substitute *Granola* for *Picnicker* - you'll be fine.

HAMMER - A TOOL USED TO ALTER THE SHAPE OF YOUR THUMB.

HYGIENE ITEM - ANYTHING MEANT TO CLEAN YOUR CARCASS. ALMOST ALL are too heavy to carry *Camping*.

ICE - WHAT THE LAKE FEELS LIKE WHEN YOU REALLY WANT TO SWIM. ALSO what your body needs for at least a week after *Camping*.

INSTANT MACARONI AND CHEESE - POOR MAN'S *DEVILED EGGS*.

. . .

LANTERN - MOSQUITO MAGNET.

LONG HANDLES - INSULATED UNDERWEAR. USED FOR SOAKING UP SNOW melt or stewing you in your own juices. Only warm when it's hot outside. Usually missing when it's cold outside.

LUNCH MEAT - ANY MEAT YOU EAT FOR LUNCH... REALLY, IT'S embarrassing that I have to explain this stuff to you.

MAP - PAPER BASED NAVIGATIONAL TOOL. IGNORED UNTIL YOU RUN OUT of *T.P.*

MATCHES - SULPHUR – TIPPED STRIPS OF WOOD OR PAPER FOR COLLECTING moisture from your other *Camping* gear; also used by sailors to attract wind.

MITTENS - INSULATED FABRIC OBJECTS USED TO KEEP KNEES DRY WHILE kneeling in snow.

NAILGUN - A TOOL USED TO FASTEN YOUR FOOT TO THE FLOOR.

PARKING PERMIT - GOVERNMENT ENDORSED EXTORTION OF CAMPERS. Exorbitantly priced and never all-inclusive, they allow *Granolas* and *Politicians* to think they're managing the wilderness. Only required if you forget to buy one.

PEANUT BUTTER - EDIBLE PASTE USED FOR GLUING KIDS' MOUTHS SHUT OR sticking the *Dog* to the outside of the *Two Man Tent*. Known to attract

The Foot.

PICNICKER - SEE *SISSY*.

POLITICIAN - ELECTED OFFICIAL WHOSE ONLY PURPOSE IS WASTING MONEY and restricting the freedom of others. Often found giving vapid speeches to crowds of adoring *granolas* and *picnickers*.

POT - KITCHEN UTENSIL USED FOR WARMING FOOD, USUALLY LEFT AT HOME to make room for *Beer*. Also, a hallucinogenic drug favored by *Granolas* and *Politicians*, recently legalized in several states - which proves that *Granolas* outnumber *Backpackers* in government. *Backpackers* prefer *Beer*. And *Coffee*.

RAIN GEAR - CONCEPTUAL CLOTHING MEANT TO KEEP THE WEARER DRY. Less effective than lingerie on a linebacker.

SASQUATCH - LARGE, HAIRY PRIMATE THOUGHT TO INHABIT THE FORESTS OF the Pacific Northwest. Believed by some (myself included) to be a man eater. Also known as Bigfoot, or to his friends, simply *The Foot*. Squirrels, birds, chipmunks, deer, and the wind are all quite adept at imitating *The Foot*, especially when you're alone at night in the woods and the only weapon you have in camp is a can opener and some leftover *Deviled Eggs*.

SAUSAGE - BREAKFAST OF CHAMPIONS. CAN BE EATEN COLD OR HOT, depending on desperation level. Known to attract *Dogs*, unprepared *Backpackers*, and *The Foot*. Really good *Sausage* is worth the risk of being eaten by *The Foot* - especially if you just finished an average *Day Hike*.

. . .

SCREWDRIVER - A TOOL USED TO CHISEL WOOD.

SHOOTING GLASSES - TARGET PRACTICE. ALSO KNOWN AS SHOOTING bottles. Actual glasses for your face are too expensive and heavy to carry *Camping*. You won't need them anyway because, well, see *Ammunition*.

SISSY - ANYONE OF TIMID BEARING OR QUEASY CONSTITUTION. ALSO, anyone who avoids danger for no reason other than it's dangerous. *Granolas, Picnickers* and *Politicians* are prime examples.

SKEETER - MOSQUITO. ALSO A DECENT NICKNAME FOR A SKINNY NERVOUS person.

SKEETER DOPE - SEE *BUG SPRAY*. ALSO WHAT YOU CALL *SKEETER* WHEN he goes *Skinny Dipping*.

SKINNY DIPPING - SWIMMING SANS CLOTHING. ALWAYS PERFORMED BY A *Dip*. Almost never performed by a skinny one.

SLEEPING BAG - AN INSULATED FABRIC BAG USED FOR SLEEPING, BUT probably more effective as an earwig trap.

SOAP - LUXURY *HYGIENE ITEM*; TOO HEAVY TO CARRY *CAMPING*. DON'T even think about it.

· · ·

SON OF A..! - World's greatest curse words. Biting off the curse at the end of the phrase lets everybody know what you're thinking, without making you a cusser-mouth in the process.

SPAM - Nitrite-infused death in a can. Considered a delicacy in Hawaii. Considered an atrocity everywhere else.

Sponge - Harmless sea creatures that have nothing to do with *Camping*. Why do you ask?

Stirring Spoon - Index finger. The real spoon got left at home to make more room for *Beer*.

Stooge - See *Doof*. Also, any one of the greatest comedic actors of our time, known collectively as the The Three Stooges.

Sunscreen - Mythical protection against sunburn. Required by Mommy if kids are going *Camping* with you. Attracts *Skeeters*, *The Foot*, and rain.

Swirlie - Verb: Shoving someone's head in the toilet and flushing it. Noun: The twisted, pointy hairdo that results from application of the verb.

Tighty-Whities - White cotton underwear designed to humiliate the wearer by riding up at inopportune times. Most glow in the dark when pants are not worn over them. This makes it easier for *The Foot* to find you after you panic and abandon your *Two Man Tent* at night. Fluorescent qualities are diminished by recent consumption of *Deviled*

Eggs.

T.P. - Luxury *Hygiene Item*. If you forget it at home and get desperate, you can always substitute your *Tighty-Whities*. You didn't want to glow in the dark, anyway.

Toothpaste - *Hygiene Item* used to clean teeth and prevent cavities. Too heavy to bring *Camping*. Use *Beer* instead.

Two Man Raft - Something used on water excursions to keep one's drinks afloat. Accommodates two men only in the catalog, or if neither of them minds drowning.

Two Man Tent - A Ziploc bag with poles. Accommodates two men only if they are stacked on top of each other and folded in thirds.

Watch This - Famous Last Words. Almost always uttered flippantly just prior to the Crack of Doom.

Zipper - Longitudinal fabric fastener engineered to lock you in your *Sleeping Bag* at the worst possible moment; i.e., when your bladder realizes it can't hold out until dawn, or when *The Foot* is stomping around behind your *Two Man Tent*.

While this list is hardly complete, it is a good start on the road to understanding my family's sense of humor. With any luck, this knowledge will keep you from walking away from a conversation with one of us muttering to yourself, "I don't get it...."

2

PERFECTLY GOOD GRISTLE

I POKED SUSPICIOUSLY AT THE AMORPHOUS MASS ON MY DINNER PLATE, wishing I hadn't eaten all my boiled potatoes. Boiled potatoes are perfect for burying things under.

"Eat it, young man," my mother said, glaring at me over the top of her glasses. "That's perfectly good gristle."

My stomach did a somersault. "It's hard as a rock! I'll break a tooth off, or something!"

"You should be glad you have teeth to chew with," she said. "Now, pipe down and finish your dinner."

Twenty minutes later, I was still gnawing on the so-called 'perfectly good gristle,' no doubt grinding my perfectly good teeth perfectly flat in the process. *Pretty soon, I'm only gonna be able to eat grass with the cows, if she makes me keep this up,* I thought. Finally, Mom got tired of waiting around for me to finish. She took her plate to the sink and moved into the living room. I jumped up from the table. "I'm gonna take out the trash now, Mom," I hollered.

"Did you eat your gristle??" She demanded.

"Mmmph<*choke*>hmmm," I lied, barely making it to the garbage can before my gag reflex kicked in. I spit the chunk of titanium tissue into the can, yanked out the bag, and ran for the back door, gulping fresh air as I burst outside. My brother Rico was practicing riding his unicycle in the driveway.

"Didja choke it down?" he asked, wobbling after me.

"Heck, no," I muttered. "I just about lost it toward the end, but then she got up to watch Jeopardy. I managed to spit it in the garbage before she saw me."

"Sissy," Rico sneered. "If it was me, I'da just swallowed it - instead of whining about it all night."

"Don't give me that," I said, stuffing the garbage bag into the rusty can behind the garage. "You've got such a weak stomach, you can barely stand to drink out of your own glass more than once. If you ever actually got served a chunk of gristle, you'd be crying and sucking your thumb under the table. Mom always gives you the best part of the pot roast."

"That's 'cuz she loves me more than you. But, you're wrong - there is no 'best part' on a pot roast. *Every* part of a pot roast is vile."

NOW DON'T START THINKING THAT MY MOTHER WAS CRUEL AND GAVE US food unfit for human consumption. That would be inaccurate.

She wasn't cruel.

She also couldn't cook, which led her to serve many things that we *assumed* were unfit for human consumption. Surrounded by twelve ravenous kids, her daily routine could easily have consisted of one continuous meal prep with no discernible break between actual meals, but she found ways to make the job easier. Every time she cooked, she would focus on quantity over quality - pot roast and boiled potatoes was such a common dinner at our house, I can scarcely remember any others.

We'd have pot roast and boiled potatoes on Monday night, followed by leftover pot roast and refried boiled potatoes on Tuesday night. Wednesday morning we'd have refried boiled potato pancakes, and Wednesday's lunch would be dried out pot roast sandwiches. By

Thursday evening, enough of Monday's dinner would have been choked down to necessitate cooking a new pot roast and boiling fresh potatoes - starting the cycle all over again.

Yum.

My parents were very frugal, so they always looked for the least expensive everything. This included pot roast - the cuts Mom bought were always the 'butcher's special' - meaning they were marked way down because even the local zoo refused to take them. That wouldn't stop Mom. She'd come home with a hunk of meat that was mostly tendons, cartilage and fat. Then she'd stick it in the oven at about 800 degrees for four hours. Add twenty pounds of potatoes boiled in our rickety pressure cooker, and voila! Dinner is served!

Because she grew up in the Great Depression, Mom refused to countenance any waste whatsoever. The fact that starving hyenas couldn't chew through the gristle in her pot roasts meant nothing to her - you just didn't waste food, and if you happened to have more gristle on your plate than meat, well, you'd better get busy chewing.

Her cooking, er, innovations weren't limited to dinner, either. On mornings that we had no thrice-leftover boiled potatoes to make pancakes, we would get oatmeal. But this oatmeal didn't come from the breakfast aisle in the grocery store - it didn't even come from the grocery store. *Our* oatmeal came from the farm and feed store - rolled oats in forty pound bags that were stacked on a pallet right next to the chicken feed.

We'd go in to get some bales of hay, or a spool of barbed wire or some other farm supplies, and the clerk would ask as he rung up the purchase, "Can I getcha anything else today, ma'am?"

Mom would do some quick math in her head, calculating instantly how much was left in the budget after buying six bales of hay, 500 feet of barbed wire and some laxative for a constipated cow. "Whyyy... I suppose we'd better get another bag of oatmeal," she'd say, exasperated.

"Sorry ma'am," the clerk would apologize. "We don't carry oatmeal. All we have is forty pound bags of rolled oats. You know - horse feed."

Mom fixed the clerk in a stern gaze over the top of her glasses. "That's what I mean. Perfectly good oatmeal. Just toss a bag on top of the hay bales, next to the bovine laxative."

"No problem," the clerk said as he shouldered a bag of oats. "How many horses do you have?"

"None," Mom said, glancing sideways at me. "But we do have a couple of stubborn asses."

"What?" I asked, not sure if I should be offended.

The rolled oats didn't produce the smooth consistency most people associate with oatmeal. Instead, they were lumpier than ten miles of bad road, and about every third bite concealed several sharp oat hulls that would randomly try to jam themselves into your gums. If you got one stuck against your tooth, it would cling there tenaciously until the tooth fell out - which often happened at dinner that same night, while you were gnawing on some perfectly good gristle.

ANOTHER STAPLE AT OUR HOUSE WAS POWDERED MILK. THIS WAS purchased in large boxes at a local warehouse. You would take some of the powder and mix it with water, stirring until the biggest chunks had dissolved or sunk to the bottom of the pitcher. The resulting liquid was thinner than dishwater, a sickly hue of bluish-grey, and tasted vaguely like chalk. I remember clearly the first time I was allowed to spend the night at a friend's house, and we had real milk - on real cereal - for breakfast.

"What's that?" I asked my friend's mom as she poured cereal into a bowl for me.

"It's Cap'n Crunch," she said.

"What's THAT?" I asked as she poured a thick, snow-white liquid over the cereal.

"It's... milk," she said.

I was a little suspicious, until I took a bite. *Ohhh... This must be what Heaven tastes like...*

The next morning, I sat staring at my bowl of horse feed drowned in dishwater. *Blecch*, I thought. The real thing had ruined me for cheap substitutes.

ONCE, MOM DID TRY TO MAKE A FANCY DISH FOR US. ONCE. IT WAS supposed to be something called Broccoli Normandy, which is made with chopped broccoli, cauliflower and carrots cooked in a lemon-zested cream sauce. Sounds harmless - even tasty, right?

Wrong.

I was young at the time of the incident, so I'm not sure exactly where the recipe jumped the track, but what ended up in our bowls was NOT Broccoli Normandy. I'm pretty sure it's impossible to make lemon-zested cream sauce by substituting apple cider vinegar for lemon juice and powdered milk for cream. The dish Mom served that night would have made Julia Child roll over in her grave - and she wasn't even dead yet. As it was, Mom's Broccoli Normandy was so horrible, Mrs. Child probably sensed a disturbance in The Force and suffered a bad case of indigestion.

Mom plunked our steaming, smelly bowls in front of us. We all recoiled. No one reached for a spoon.

"Well?" she demanded. "Get eating! That's perfectly good Broccoli Normandy!"

I looked at my bowl, half afraid that my perfectly good Broccoli Normandy would grab me by my perfectly good throat and choke the life out of me. Rico suppressed a gag, and Lauralynn fled the table with a hand over her mouth. Jinty held her nose as a tear rolled down her cheek.

Mom was fuming. "NONE of you are leaving this table until you eat!" She stormed out.

Retching noises echoed from the bathroom.

Jinty turned green.

Rico looked like he was going to faint.

As the youngest and smallest, I would almost *never* turn down food. At our house, if you didn't wolf your food down like you were starving, you'd be too late to get seconds. The food was never very tasty, but I was *always* hungry - so I usually choked down whatever was placed in front of me in hopes of getting seconds and having enough to satisfy the constant gnawing in my stomach. My siblings knew this, and often pawned their inedibles off on me. They would furtively get my attention, desperately avoiding my Dad's line of sight, and the exchange would go something like this:

Revolted Sibling (spoken in a soundless whisper): *"MP! Hey! MP!"*

Me (Raising an eyebrow as I stuff my mouth with boiled potatoes): *"What?"*

Revolted Sibling: (Points discreetly at unwanted food on plate, raises eyebrow).

Me: (Jerk eyebrows up and down, smile while gnawing perfectly good gristle).

The food in question would then be smuggled off the plate and passed carefully across several kids' laps to me, and I would make it disappear. I was a closer of sorts at the dinner table - the clean-up batter in a game of revolting food baseball.

But even I drew the line at Mom's Broccoli Normandy. This pungent, soggy, greyish mass was more than even I could take. Rico tried to get my attention.

"MP! Hey! MP!" he rasped at me, desperate.

I made a point of ignoring him, staring straight ahead at the sweat forming on Jinty's brow.

"MP!" he tried a little volume this time, barely audible, but twice as urgent.

I clamped my jaw shut and shook my head, the motion barely perceptible but the meaning crystal clear. *You're on your own, buddy.*

More retching and whimpering came from the bathroom. Now Jinty was a sickly yellow-green and had a vacant stare on her face. Rico started moaning softly, wavering back and forth in his chair. The situation was rapidly approaching critical mass. Rico was going to do a face plant in his bowl at any moment, and then Jinty would regain consciousness long enough to lose her lunch - and I was directly in her line of fire. I panicked, and took the only way out I could think of.

I took a bite.

The hair on the back of my neck curled up, and my eyes instantly started watering. A muscle on my jaw started spasming wildly.

Mom suddenly walked back into the room. "Why aren't you finished yet?" she growled at Jinty.

No! I thought. *Don't wake her up!!*

Jinty's eyes were glazed over, her pupils dilated.

"I think I'm gonna puke," Rico mumbled. Mom spun on him.

"You'd better NOT puke, young man! I will not tolerate you wasting perfectly good food! Money doesn't grow on trees, you know!"

Meanwhile, my jaw was in the middle of a grand mal seizure. My hand went limp and my spoon clattered to the table, splattering Rico with soggy bits of broccoli. Or maybe it was Normandy. Either way, it caused his Adam's apple to bob up and down at about 4500 RPM, and his entire upper body started to convulse. I couldn't take it any more. Leaping up from the table, I knocked my chair over and spilled my powdered milk in Rico's lap.

"SIT DOWN!!" Mom hollered at me as I fled. She swung a kick at me, but the cat got tangled with her feet and almost knocked her down. I accelerated, overshooting the turn into the bathroom and crashing into the doorjamb. Lauralynn was prostrate on the floor, faking death. I tripped over her leg and fell head first into the toilet bowl, almost giving myself a swirlie.

I don't know exactly how Jinty and Rico escaped eating their dinner that night, but I do know that Mom never attempted to practice haute cuisine on us again. Pot roast and potatoes were back on the menu.

THE FUNNY THING IS, LATER IN LIFE WHILE BUYING MY OWN GROCERIES, I priced powdered milk - just out of curiosity. It was almost ten times as expensive as real milk! I knew that we were directed by our parents to mix our powdered milk thinner than recommended on the box in order to make it go farther, but even mixing it at half strength, we were still paying five times as much. This didn't gibe at all with my parent's frugality policy. There had to be some explanation.

If they hadn't forced us to drink the vile swill out of thrift, then what was it? Maybe they were trying to toughen up our palates, just in case we ran into a famine later in life and had to drink dishwater to wash down our perfectly good gristle.

Or…

…maybe they were a just a *little* cruel…

3

MT. MCLOUGHLIN (THE HARD WAY)

My brother Jethro is a self-styled adventurer.

I say that because there weren't any real adventurers in the history of exploration and conquest whose style he liked, so he invented his own. Jethro enjoys planning new and more difficult ways to perform mundane recreational outings, just to make them more interesting (and, in the process, imminently more dangerous) than they would normally be. While the great Antarctic explorer Sir Ernest Shackleton was known for his ability to bring all his men home alive from the worst disasters, Jethro prefers to drag as many people as possible, willing or otherwise, toward disaster's very brink. Whether or not anyone actually comes home alive is a minor and uninteresting sidebar to his idea of an otherwise noteworthy adventure.

With this unnerving tendency in mind, I found myself one fine summer day listening to Jethro plot an excursion to the top of Mt. McLoughlin in Southern Oregon's Cascade Mountains. Now, to anyone familiar with the region and its various summits, McLoughlin is by no means a difficult climb. It rises to just under 9,500 feet above sea level, with the trailhead starting on the high side of 5,000 feet. For someone in good shape on a summer day of favorable weather, the peak can be conquered before lunch, with time left over to hike back down to a nearby lake for a relaxing dip before dark. Of course, that assumes favorable weather and the use of the well-marked trail. Since Jethro had spent a great deal of his youth and early adulthood stomping through the national forests near our hometown in search of ever greater adventures, he'd already climbed McLoughlin via the approved Forest Service trail many times, and was suitably bored with the route to necessitate a different tack.

"I aint taking the yak route again," he announced. "That's for sissies."

"So explain to me again why you're not taking it?" I asked.

"Shaddap, you. Here's what we need to do." He unfolded his Forest Service map of the area. "Here's the trail," he said, pointing at the gently sloped eastern ridge. "Here's where we're going." He pointed directly at the steepest part of the mountain, the bowl on the northeast side. "And here's the best part, stoop. I found this at a yard sale." He held up a beat up 1-wood golf club. "We can use this to smack golf balls into orbit when we get to the top. It'll be great!"

Let me note here that Jethro is no golfer. He's never set foot on a golf course, except for the chance fairway crossing as he stumbled out of the woods in the combined pursuit of adventure and the last place he saw the car. I, on the other hand, enjoy golf immensely. I am no good at it, but enjoy it nonetheless. I have my own clubs, shoes, pull-cart, and most importantly to Jethro, a large supply of weathered golf balls that ride around in my bag for use when shooting anywhere near a water hazard. Which explained why Jethro invited me along.

"See, we'll use your thrashed range balls and my sweet driver, and we'll be able to say we golfed McLoughlin! Cool, huh?"

"Yeah. Cool." I was skeptical, to say the least. The idea of slapping a golf ball into the next county from a 9,500 foot tee box was tempting, but because it was Jethro's idea, I knew something had to be wrong with it.

"C'mon, stooge," he said. Jethro often refers to me in the derogatory sense, in a lame attempt to cover up shameless admiration. "You can't possibly tell me you don't want to go. Would you rather hang out with the huddled masses on a golf course, or have some adventure with me?"

"I dunno," I said. "Would the huddled masses get to huddle over burgers and beers after their round, or would they be rushed to the emergency room for frostbite and exposure? Tough choice..."

"Sissy."

"When do we leave?"

"Next weekend."

"You're driving."

"Cool. Maybe you're not a sissy, after all."

SATURDAY MORNING FOUND US AT OUR JUMPING OFF SPOT, A campground scarcely five miles from the mountain. As we adjusted our day packs and strategically placed water bottles and candy bars within easy reach, Jethro's brother-in-law Rooney pulled into the campground. Rooney owns a Tae Kwon Do school in town, and makes his livelihood by teaching young children to kick each other in the head without damaging their feet. Once a year, he guides his young charges into the woods for a day of running amok, practicing attacks and ambushes on each other and any hikers unlucky enough to get in their way. Rooney's truck had barely rolled to a stop before several young boys clambered from the cab and proceeded to dash to and fro about the campground. Rooney got out and sauntered over, wearing his best cynical sneer.

"What are you clods doing out here? Ya lost?"

Jethro grinned. "I don't get lost, sap. Occasionally re-routed, but never lost."

"Riiiighhht. Looks like you're lost to me. Nearest golf course is thirty miles away."

Jethro looked at the golf club in his hand. "We don't need no golf course. We're gonna drive balls off the top of McLoughlin."

"Ha!" Rooney scoffed. "That makes you lost *and* stupid! You dopes wanna climb McLoughlin, the trailhead is about ten miles south of here. Don't feel bad, though. Being lost is better than wasting a day of your lives on senseless climbing." Rooney has no use for mountain climbing of any kind, unless there is a lake at the top full of starving fish.

One of his students scampered up and snapped to attention, trying to catch his breath.

"Sir, excuse me, sir, but what will we be using for weapons?"

I looked at Jethro. "Let's go, dope. I'd rather get lost and die on the mountain than be used as a punching bag for a ten year old." I slung my pack over my shoulder.

"Can I have your truck when you don't make it back?" Rooney asked Jethro.

"Funny," Jethro said. "You stay away from my truck. Keep your little minions away from it, too."

Rooney muttered something about better uses for a golf club, then walked away, barking at his students like a deranged drill sergeant.

WE WERE BARELY TEN YARDS FROM THE TRUCK WHEN I NOTICED THE FIRST flaw in Jethro's plan. Apparently, he is a firm believer in the maxim, "He who plans the trip is automatically the leader." I had made the mistake of not recognizing this before he could attempt to lead me - which gave him the idea that it was true.

We were walking side by side, Jethro on my left. For some reason, he kept walking slightly right of straight ahead, herding me to the right and driving us more downhill than up. At first, I simply angled to the right too, but it quickly became obvious that his leading would get us nowhere fast. Not wanting to walk in circles all day, and knowing that the summit of McLoughlin was a much more desirable goal than the brink of disaster, I voiced my concern.

"Where are you going, clodhopper?"

"Where does it look like I'm going? I'm *going* to teach you how to hit a golf ball off a mountain."

"Too bad the mountain is to the left, huh?" I immediately took an emergency vote of one and elected myself the leader. My first official act was to veer back to the left, which had the effect of intersecting Jethro's personal space.

He suddenly realized there had been a mutiny, and I hadn't invited him.

"Idiot, you're going the wrong way!"

"I know where I'm going," I said, "and you're not pointed at it! You keep trying to herd me to the right, which, oh, look! ...happens to be downhill! I've got golf balls to hit, and I'm not doing it from low elevation. Any fool knows that if you want to climb mountains, the first thing you need to do is GAIN ALTITUDE!"

Faced with this indisputable bit of logic, Jethro sunk into a pout, interrupted by subtle, repeated attempts to veer to the right. I ignored his foolishness, and continued to steer him to the left. When we finally broke out of the trees a mere twenty yards from the ridge line we were looking for, he tried to take credit for our success.

"Good thing I was in charge," he said. "You'd probably be dying of exposure right now if you hadn't had me to guide you."

"Oh, please," I scoffed. "If it wasn't for MY innate sense of direction, we would have walked in a forty mile circle before Rooney's junior ninja league slaughtered us ten feet from the truck."

"Quit yer yapping," he said. "We still got most of a mountain to climb." He looked up at our path to the summit. I immediately realized this was going to be somewhat less enjoyable than playing eighteen holes of golf without a power cart. We were confronted by roughly a thousand boulders, each the size of an average house, and none with any easy way around. Beyond that was a ridiculously steep rock slope covered with pea-shaped gravel. When you took a step on the gravel, it would stay in place just long enough for you to put all your weight on your foot - then it would explode from under your boot, so you could fall right back to the pile of nice soft boulders below.

"You moron!" I called to Jethro as I unwrapped my kidneys from a big rock for the third time. "This is the stupidest route on the mountain! We're gonna get killed climbing this!"

"I tried to tell ya we shouldn't come this way," Jethro said as he pulled some gravel from his teeth. "It's all your fault."

"My fault?!? I didn't want to climb this stupid mountain at all, much less climb it on this road to nowhere! Why do I let you talk me into things like this, anyway?"

"Cuz you're stupid, and I'm your hero," he said. "That's what hero worship gets you. Now, quit your belly-achin' and lift this boulder offa my spleen."

WE KEPT STRUGGLING UPWARD, BUT OUR INTENSE CONCENTRATION ON OUR present obstacle took our attention away from the gathering clouds in the sky overhead - mostly because it's impossible to keep one eye on your feet and one on the sky, even when both eyes are bugged out that far.

When we finally dragged ourselves to the crest of the next ridge, the wind had picked up and the weather was well on its way from warm and enjoyable to cold and scary. As we sat down to drink some water and eat a few candy bars, the howling wind threatened to rip my hat from my head.

"Holy mackerel!" I hollered, grabbing my hat just in time. I ducked under a scrawny tree that was growing right out of a rock, its puny limbs stretched almost a whole foot off the ground. It offered a little shelter from the wind, but that didn't matter much when the rain started. As the ninety mile-per-hour wind drove raindrops into my flesh, I wished I'd never bought any tank tops or shorts, which, except for my boots and my favorite hat (now yanked firmly down around my ears) was all I had on. I yanked open my pack and realized with horror that in my haste to get away from Rooney's little thugs, I had left my sweatshirt on the seat of the truck.

My teeth chattered like a machine gun. I stared, disbelieving, at the frighteningly steep route ahead. Then I looked over at Jethro.

He was busily chewing a fried chicken drumstick, giggling like a loon.

I started to question my own sanity as I watched his steadily erode into the freezing air. He was obviously enjoying this! I have to admit, being atop a precarious windswept ridge where no one else dared go *was* pretty cool, but I draw the line at maniacal giggling.

Jethro gnawed the last bit of chicken, then tossed the bone into the air. The wind snatched it away like a dust bunny into a shop-vac. "This is great!" he shouted into the gale. "No picnickers ever came this way, I bet! WOOHOO!!"

"I'd rather be with twenty picnickers than one raving lunatic," I said.

"WHAT?" he shouted back.

"I SAID, YOU'RE A RAVING…oh, never mind." It was impossible to make myself heard. Besides, he'd started giggling again.

Just then, the rain abruptly stopped. It was like somebody turned off a giant faucet. The sun broke through the clouds, and the wind died down to a gentle shriek.

"See?" Jethro crowed. "I told ya this was great!"

"Yeah, great," I said. "I've always wondered what freezer burn feels like. Now I can tell my friends."

———

WE SET OUT AGAIN. I LET JETHRO TAKE THE LEAD, BECAUSE I DIDN'T WANT him to shove me into an abyss with his constant swerving. I let him get far enough ahead that his erratic turns would only result in zigzags on his part, not free-falls on mine. We hiked across a steep face peppered with more loose gravel, followed by a turn directly up an even steeper face covered with snow.

It was about 300 yards to the top of the snow field, with no way around. We kicked steps into the melting snow, punched handholds with our fists, and made like a couple of nervous frostbitten crabs skittering up a concrete sea wall with a hurricane at our backs. Once above the snow field, we found ourselves protected from the incessant wind by the huge pinnacle of rock that is the most readily identifiable feature of McLoughlin from far away.

I caught myself wishing *I* was far away.

We climbed along a crevasse left between the pinnacle and a receding glacier, and once past that came into full view of the summit not far above. We occasionally caught sight of herds of picnickers on the ridge to the south of us, scrambling to get to the top before their supply of deviled eggs spoiled.

About a hundred yards below the summit, the ridge opened out wide enough to allow me to pass Jethro without fear of being knocked off into the void below, and I reclaimed my rightful place in the lead. As I dragged myself over the last pile of rocks below the final summit ridge, I surprised a group of picnickers. They gaped at me, thinking I must be some sort of madman to have climbed up such a dangerous route.

Then Jethro dragged himself onto the trail behind me, giggling.

The picnickers fled down the mountain, sandals slapping the trail like Moe slapping Shemp's forehead. Suddenly, I found it impossible to stifle a giggle of my own.

"Sissies," Jethro said. "They obviously don't know a real adventurer when they see one."

"Maybe not, but they do know when they see a psycho. Good thing I brought you along to scare 'em away."

We continued up the ridge, finally reaching the summit a few minutes later. The view was incredible, and the wind had stopped altogether. I was feeling rather proud of myself when a sudden thought struck me:

Mountains are made of rocks.

Rocks are hard.

Golf courses are soft and green.

I hadn't brought any tees.

Even if I had brought tees along, there would have been no place to stick them amongst the assorted boulders at the summit. There was no soft dirt anywhere - just jagged rocks.

At that moment, I thought I was going to have a fit. All this way, risking my life with my lunatic brother, just to hit golf balls, and now there was no way to tee off without shattering the head of the club on a chunk of granite! I was beside myself.

I walked around the ruins of an old lookout tower that sits atop the mountain, looking for a quiet place to sulk. Hidden behind the rubble, I came across a beautiful sight: a small patch of snow, right on the summit, that had somehow avoided melting in the warm sunshine. I bent down, pinched my fingers together, and molded a perfect golf tee in the snow.

Now, I had something to giggle about.

"Hey, Jethro," I called. "Get over here and bring that crummy driver with ya!" I dropped my pack and rummaged in it for golf balls.

For the next few minutes, we took turns crushing drives off into space. The thin air and sheer 1,000 foot drop off the north side of the mountain allowed us to hit farther than Jack Nicklaus on his best day. By the time we ran out of golf balls, we were both laughing uncontrollably. Then we noticed a man, wearing a beret, peering over the ruined lookout foundation and watching us in disgust. Obviously, he had never played golf.

We ignored him and found a spot to relax and soak up some sun. I leaned against a big rock and contemplated the more important questions facing mankind, such as, "The Meaning of it All"; "Is There Really a Bigfoot?"; and "What would a golf ball hit from 9,500 feet do to someone climbing a mountain via an uncharted route below it?"

Then another pack of picnickers came up the trail, oohing and ahhing and taking pictures. I snapped out of my reverie.

"Time to go, dope," I told Jethro. "This place is gettin' too crowded."

"Yup," he said. "Let's take the trail to that point about a quarter mile down, then we'll follow the ridge into the trees right back to the truck." He pointed at a knife-edge ridge to the southeast.

"Okay by me. Anything's better than the route we came in on."

Or not.

The area between McLoughlin's northeast and southeast ridges is a large, steep bowl filled with snow and rocks. It spreads out wide at the bottom and points directly at Fourmile Lake in the distance, which is where we had left the truck. Jethro found a spot where one of the snow fields in the bowl reached up to the knife edge of the ridge.

"Watch this!" he said. "Shortcut!" Then, using his golf club as a brake, he dropped onto his backside in the snow at the top of the bowl and immediately shot out of sight.

I stared in shock at the space he had just vacated, thinking he'd finally slipped into total insanity. He'd taken our only golf club.

I crept close to the edge, expecting to hear a long wavering scream as he pitched out of control to his death on the rocks below. There was nothing but the wind.

And a faint giggle.

With no club of my own for a brake, I had to take the ridge to the bottom. Disgusted, I hurried off. I couldn't allow Jethro to beat me to the bottom, even if he got killed getting there.

As I picked up my pace, the ridge got progressively steeper, the rocks got looser, and I quickly found myself running out of control. I leaped boulders and small trees, picking up speed and momentum with every stride. Close behind me was an ever increasing avalanche of gravel and scree that threatened to bury me alive if I dared to stop.

"Idiot!" I snarled, bouncing off of a tree. "He'd better not die, 'cuz I'm gonna kill him!"

The idea of Jethro sliding gleefully down a snow field on his derriere, beating me to the bottom of the bowl, made my liver bile percolate. Not to mention, he had the keys to the truck. If he got off the mountain first, he'd probably forget why he was there and head home without me. I ran faster, ricocheting off obstacles left and right. My boots were packed full of rocks, stickers, and small woodland creatures, but I kept going.

I met up with Jethro about a quarter of a mile farther along, as he picked his way through the beginning of a field of boulders at the bottom of the bowl. The jury is still out as to who chose the best route. The only similarity between the two was that Jethro and I both ended up a little wet, he from sliding on the snow, and me from bleeding all over myself.

WE PRESSED ON. AS WE WOULD FIND OUT LATER AFTER SCRUTINIZING A map, our route took us slightly farther south than we needed to go. Since our general heading was eastbound, getting too far south could only have been caused by steadily veering to the right. My preoccupation with my rock filled boots must have prevented me from keeping Jethro on course, and we ended up smack in the middle of a huge collection of bogs and mosquito infested swamps.

"You clown!" I hollered as I slapped myself in the forehead, killing a dozen mosquitos in one swat. "You got us off course again!"

"No I didn't!" Jethro snapped back. He had so many bugs caught in his hair it looked like he was growing dreadlocks. "You were leading!"

A single mosquito flew straight into my right ear. "Aaigghh!!" I started spinning in circles and slapping myself. "They're gonna suck us dry if we don't get outta here!

I have never seen so many mosquitoes, so hungry, and so large, all in one place at one time. They came in droves, ignoring our flailing and slapping, determined to suck what little blood we had left. The buzzing was so loud, it was like sitting in the middle of a runway during the National Remote Control Airplane Derby.

Jethro looked at me, slapped himself upside the head, and ran. I yanked my boot from a mud hole and followed, slapping myself silly all the way. Half an hour later, and about two quarts low each, we burst from the underbrush near the campground, started the truck, and fled for our lives.

As we sped away we passed Rooney, relaxing in a lawn chair near the lake. We waved, but he just stared. He was probably wondering why two giant, hairy red welts were driving around in Jethro's truck.

Because we escaped with our lives, Jethro is no doubt already planning some new backwoods insanity aimed at matching my age with my life expectancy. As his brother, I feel sort of obligated to go along to keep him from killing himself, but the idea gets harder to stomach as his plans call for plunging into ever deeper wilderness, snow, and impenetrable clouds of carnivorous insects. Maybe after the cuts heal, and I dig the last of the mosquito carcasses out of my hair, and after that funny facial tic subsides... But then again - the brink of disaster looks a lot better from a safe distance.

4
PILLOW BOXING

I GREW UP IN A LARGE FAMILY, THE YOUNGEST OF TWELVE CHILDREN. BY today's standards, that seems an abnormally large number, but it never seemed to phase my parents much. I suspect they are both made of much sterner stuff than people of younger generations. The size of our family didn't seem unusual to me either, and I could never quite understand the shock on people's faces when they heard how many of us there were. Later in life I would use the information just to get a jaw drop or dumbfounded look out of a new acquaintance (much to my satisfaction), but beyond that, being from such a large clan felt perfectly normal.

The reason I never felt any different is that I had nothing else to compare my life to. The closest thing I had was re-runs of 'The Brady Bunch', which never made much sense to me anyway. I could never figure out how a mere six children could possibly cause so much chaos and noise in a home, and still be sickeningly sweet to each other by the end of the half hour show. The Bradys had half as many kids as we did, and twice the confusion. I recall our house as being a place of discipline and reverent silence, at least as long as Dad was at home. I've seen episodes of 'The Brady Bunch' where the father comes home after a long day at work, only to be surrounded by a brood of shrieking children, running circles around him like a tribe of enraged savages preparing for a war party.

My father would never have stood for such nonsense. When Dad was around, we cut him a wide berth for as long as it took to figure out what kind of mood he was in, plus ten minutes. If he was in a good mood, we could relax a bit and go about our business in a quiet and orderly way. If he was in a bad mood, we did our best to vanish into thin air until he left for work the next day. This was to ensure that his bad mood and our bad luck would not cross paths. Dad had a short fuse, to say the least, and all of us were loath to expose it to flame.

Keeping this in mind, let me say that there were always instances where someone's caution and/or common sense would lapse, and we would commit some foolish act and get on Dad's bad side. Mostly, these occurrences would be short and not altogether sweet, swiftly culminating in Dad showing us the error of our ways in any of several very convincing manners. He never failed to find ways to immediately restore order, putting us quickly in our place and increasing our personal vigilance for a week or two. At rare times, however, one or more of us would completely lose our minds, ignore all warning signals of the coming storm, and plummet headlong into Dad's temper. The short-lived but entertaining sport of Pillow Boxing was the centerpiece of just such an event.

My brother Rico and I shared a bedroom for many years of our youth. Being forced to live in such close proximity to my brother was not exactly my cup of tea, and since Rico is four years older than me, he liked it even less. We managed to get along though, and at times even had fun with the arrangement. Considering the size of our family and the high cost and resulting scarcity of real toys, we were compelled to come up with creative ways to entertain ourselves.

One evening, we were hiding out in our room from our parents and some of their friends who were over for coffee and idle chit-chat. We knew that causing a disruption of the social activities would be met with immediate and harsh reprisals. This point was driven home by past experience, coupled with a stern glance from my mother just before the guests arrived.

We retreated to our room.

Once there, we looked around for something to do. We had tried several things with no visible effect on the settling boredom, when a thoughtful look came over Rico's face. As I tried to figure out what he was thinking, he abruptly cuffed me upside the head with a small throw pillow he'd found on my bed. We had two of these pillows in our room, each about a foot square, covered in a kind of satiny polyester material. I have no idea where they came from or why we had them in our room - they looked like left over decorations from a swinger party at Club 54 - but I digress.

Rico had discovered that by squeezing all the stuffing out of one corner, the pillow could be firmly held by grasping the remaining cover material, and then could be swung with considerable force. Actually, I was the one who first discovered and fully appreciated the force of a well swung pillow, but we won't nit-pick here. After shooing the little birds and stars from around my head, I heard Rico saying something about what good boxing gloves the pillows would make. Being still young and naïve, I agreed, and armed myself with the other pillow. We started to circle the room, facing off like scrawny versions of George Foreman and Muhammad Ali.

I feinted left as he tried a jab. I slipped his offense and swung a haymaker, narrowly missing the tip of his nose. He sent a crushing blow to my ribs, then shoved me back with his empty hand and tagged me with a stout uppercut. I staggered backward and tried not to laugh out loud. Rico was already laughing hysterically, but somehow managing to keep it muffled so our parents wouldn't hear. He stopped to take a breath, and I swung a vicious overhand at his left temple. It connected with a satisfying *THWOP*, and Rico dropped to his knees, dazed and half incapacitated by a giggling fit.

The door flew open.

Dad was standing in the doorway, chest heaving with barely suppressed rage.

"You two knotheads had better *pipe down!!*" he snarled through clenched teeth. We tried to look innocent, but he wasn't buying it. "If I have to come back in here, you've both *had it!!*" His voice never climbed above conversational volume, so his guests were none the wiser to his fury. He closed the door and left us to contemplate our near-death experience.

"Guess we better find something else to do, huh?" I asked Rico, non-committal.

"Guess so." He looked at me and started snickering, trying not to laugh out loud.

"What's so funny?"

His pillow shot out, connecting with my nose and making my eyes water. Now I was trying not to laugh out loud.

What is it about being in a situation that demands restraint, that makes it so hard to restrain yourself?

I smacked him on the ear at about half strength, testing to see if I could do it silently. Rico jumped up and clubbed me over the head, making me bite my tongue.

Fight's on, fight's on.

Now we were both laughing out loud, swinging our pillows wildly in hopes of connecting with something tender and vulnerable. Rico tried to pivot away, and I hit him with a body blow that took the wind out of him. I wound up for the *coup de grâce*, but left my guard open. Rico swung with all his might, connecting with the side of my head as I waded forward. It was a perfect shot, and I swear I heard my own bell ringing. My knees buckled, and I collapsed against my bed, which slid up against the wall, making a racket like somebody had kicked a full tool box down a flight of concrete steps.

Before I had finished falling, Rico leapt into his bed and pulled the covers over his head, feigning sleep.

The door flew open again.

THIS TIME DAD DIDN'T SPEAK. I WAS STILL ON THE FLOOR, STRUGGLING TO get to my feet before the ten-count. Dad strode over, picked up my dropped pillow, and loomed above me. He waited until my vision cleared enough for me to recognize him - then he swatted me back to the ground, swinging the pillow in a furious two-handed arc like he was chopping firewood. Rico poked his head out of his covers to witness my execution, and Dad caught him with a backhand swing of the pillow that knocked him flat. Then Dad threw the pillow at my head, making it go *clonk* against the floor.

"*Go to sleep!*" he snarled. "And you're *both* gonna get it in the morning!" He stalked out and flicked off the light, leaving us in darkness.

I dragged myself off the floor and managed to crawl into bed. Rico wasn't laughing any more.

"What do you think he's gonna do to us?" I asked the darkness.

"Kill us, probably." Rico has a gift for exaggeration.

"Maybe he'll forget by tomorrow," I offered. Muffled adult laughter from the living room mocked me.

"Hey," Rico said, his voice gaining optimism. "I just remembered! Tomorrow's my birthday! He won't want to kill us on my birthday, right?"

"You, maybe," I said. "I doubt he'd mind killing *me* on your birthday." Optimism wasn't my strong suit where discipline was concerned.

Our family had an unofficial tradition of spanking the birthday boy or girl, matching the exact number of playful swats to whatever age was on the birthday card. These were always followed by creative riffs on the corporal punishment theme: A pinch to grow an inch; a sock to grow a block; a punch to grow a bunch; etc. The tradition was basically a loosely approved way for everybody to get in any shots they may have missed during the course of the previous year. The conversation might go something like this:

Aggrieved Sibling: "Remember when you broke my bike last November?"

Birthday Victim: "Uh, no. YOU broke your bike last November, when you left it behind the tractor and Dad ran over it."

Sibling: "Yeah, well, that was your fault. Here's a punch to grow a bunch." SMACK. "Oh, yeah. I almost forgot. Happy Birthday."

Nobody really liked this tradition, but nobody protested it either, because if you lobbied for more civilized behavior, you might miss your chance to get payback. Anyway, Rico was hoping that Dad would commute his sentence since it was his birthday, and let the rest of us mete out our own form of justice according to tradition. My chances of clemency, however, were less than zero. I struggled to get to sleep, tossing and turning and fretting about my coming dawn execution. When I did finally drift off, I somehow forgot about the incident.

NEXT MORNING, I WOKE UP DROOLING ON MY PILLOW. WHEN I REALIZED what I was doing, I rolled over in disgust - and rolled up against the throw pillow Dad had used to bludgeon me into submission the night before. My stomach did a somersault, and I looked over at Rico to see if he was dead yet.

"Rico! You awake?"

"I am now," he mumbled, pulling his blankets over his head. "Thanks a lot, ya dope."

"Erm, Happy Birthday?" I offered.

Rico popped up like he'd been poked with a cattle prod. "Hey, yeah! It's my birthday! Woohoo!" He started rummaging around on the floor, looking in vain for un-disgusting clothes to wear from the pile of dirty laundry that doubled as our carpeting. "It's my birthday, it's my birthday," he sang. He bent over at the waist and waved his tighty-whiteys at me, dancing and gyrating with glee. I grabbed the throw pillow and smacked him hard in the back of the knee, making his leg buckle.

"Ya moron!" I scoffed. "Don't you remember? Dad's gonna kill me and clobber you! All you're gettin' for your birthday is a whuppin'! Har!" The knowledge that I was getting a beating too didn't dampen my sudden desire to rain on Rico's parade. Gloating in your under-wear is just asking for it.

"Awww, man," Rico moaned. "What a crummy birthday!"

I swung my feet out onto the floor. "Maybe we could run away," I suggested. "We could probably live in the barn, and nobody would even miss us."

"Ya big stoop," Rico scoffed. "We can't do that. Where would we wash our clothes?"

"Who cares? We don't wash our clothes now, and it hasn't hurt us yet."

"So what will we eat?"

I thought about it. "There's a bunch of canned bean-with-bacon soup in the kitchen. We can eat that."

"How are we supposed to heat it up? There's no power in the barn, and if we light a fire in there and burn it down, somebody's gonna notice!"

"We'll eat it cold, out of the can," I said. "It's good that way."

Rico made a face. "Is there anything you won't eat? That's sick!"

"You dancing around in your tighty-whiteys is what's sick. Bean-with-bacon soup is just food."

"It oughta be dog food." Rico found a pair of grungy jeans and pulled them on. "You better get dressed," he said. "You oughta wear jeans and stuff something in the back pockets so it hurts less when Dad clobbers ya."

"He aint gonna clobber me," I said, "'cuz I'm running away to the barn. You're on your own."

Our mother's shrill 'kid-call' voice suddenly pierced the air. "RI-CO!! M-P!! Get down here!!"

We both froze. "Looks like you're too late," Rico said. "We're dead."

"Maybe not," I said. "Why would *Mom* call us down so Dad can kill us? If he was gonna do it, he'd have come in here already and killed us in our sleep. Maybe he forgot!"

"Maybe," Rico said as he pulled on a dirty t-shirt and shoved some stained socks in his back pockets. "But if Mom has to call you again, Dad'll have a reason to remember." He bolted out the door. "I'm coming, Mom!" he shouted. "MP's still asleep!"

"No I'm not!" I shrieked as I looked around frantically for socks to stuff in my pockets. I vowed to give Rico several punches to grow a bunch. I thundered down the stairs after him, yanking a t-shirt over my head and trying to zip up my pants. Mom was in the kitchen, draining hot bacon grease from a frying pan into an old coffee can.

"Can I have MP's bacon, since he slept in?" Rico asked, sidling up against Mom.

"Shut up!" I protested. "I woke up before you did! *I* should get *your* bacon!"

"Yeah, but it's *my* birthday," Rico said. "You should give me your bacon just cuzza that."

"Neither of you is getting any bacon," Mom said, plucking a slice from the pan and crunching it up as we watched. "This is mine. I just called you down here because the garbage and trash need to go out."

"Awww," we whined in stereo.

"Quit your whining and get it done before your father comes home," Mom said as she sprinkled pepper on another piece of bacon. *Dad wasn't home.*

"Uh, where's Dad?" I discreetly raised my eyebrows in Rico's direction.

"He went to have coffee with his buddies," Mom explained. "Should be back any time."

Rico glanced at me, then inclined his head toward the soup cabinet. "Okay, Mom. MP can take out the garbage, and I'll burn the trash. Where are the matches?"

My eyes got wide, and I tried to shake my head without alerting Mom.

Rico ignored me. "After we finish taking out the papers and garbage, can we play outside for a while?"

Mom breathed a sigh of apparent relief. "I don't care *what* you do - just get the garbage out and burn the papers. And don't light anything important on fire."

"I won't," Rico assured her as he shouldered past me, pausing to hiss *sotto voce* in my ear: *"Get the soup!"*

I MADE A BIG SHOW OF COLLECTING THE HOUSEHOLD GARBAGE, TRYING TO look busy without actually doing much. I kept one eye on Mom as she finished her breakfast. When she got up to refill her coffee, I managed to snatch three cans of bean-with-bacon soup from the cabinet. I fumbled with the cans, not sure where to hide them. Mom was stirring sugar into her coffee with a purpose, the spoon going *tink-tink-tink*. I knew I only had a few more *tinks* before she turned around and caught me. I tried to jam the cans in my pants pockets, but they were too big.

Tink-tink-tink.

I stuffed them up under my shirt, almost dropping one on my toe.

Tink-tink-tink.

I shoved them into my waistband, and popped the button off my jeans.

Tink-tink.

Tink.

Panicked, I let the cans fall into the full garbage bag at my feet just as Mom finished *tinking* and turned around. "Are you still diddling around with that?" She asked. "You're slower than molasses in January!" She blew on her coffee and left the room, shaking her head scornfully. I exhaled with relief and hoisted the greasy garbage bag, holding it at arm's length so it wouldn't drip something unspeakable on me.

Rico met me outside at the garbage can behind our garage. He had already set all the paper trash on fire in the empty oil drum out by the cow pasture. "What the heck took you so long?" he asked, punching me hard on the shoulder.

"Quit it!" I said, taking the lid off the garbage can. "I had to wait until she poured more coffee. I almost got caught!"

"Where's the soup, stupid?"

"In here." I opened the bag. The soup cans had worked their way down to the bottom of the pile and were covered in coffee grounds, egg shells and all manner of toxic waste.

"Bleecchh!" Rico gagged. "I aint eatin' that!"

I tried to hold my breath long enough to reach into the bag for the soup, but the stench was awful. "Oohhh, that's nasty!" I thrust the open bag at Rico. "Here - you try."

He started to protest, but stopped himself in mid-choke. Dad's car was turning into the driveway. "Here comes Dad-dy!" he said, forgetting all about the stink. I froze in place like a deer in the headlights.

FROM OUR POSITION AT THE BACK CORNER OF THE GARAGE, WE COULD ONLY see the passenger side of Dad's car as it rolled to a stop out front. We waited, hoping he wouldn't notice us as he went in the house. The car door slammed shut. We leaned a little farther around the corner, trying to gauge Dad's mood from afar. When he didn't appear, we looked at each other.

"Where'd he go?" I whispered.

"I dunno," Rico said, shrugging.

"WHADDYA DOIN' BACK HERE?!?" Dad's sudden bellow from behind made us both squeal. He must have walked around the other side of the garage, flanking us while we were focused on the frontal assault. Rico trampled me in his panic to get away. I dropped the garbage bag, spilling filth and one can of bean-with-bacon soup at Dad's feet. He picked it up, flicking a banana peel at my head.

"DADGUMMIT! Who's throwing away perfectly good soup?!?" My shoulders sagged. Even if he'd been in a good mood two seconds before, there was no way it would survive exposure to evidence of food being wasted.

LATER, AS WE SNIVELED QUIETLY IN OUR BEDS, I TRIED TO PUT THINGS IN perspective. "At least he didn't kill us," I said. I curled into a fetal position and tentatively rubbed my backside.

"Yeah, but he hacked me twice more 'cuz I had socks in my pockets!" Rico whined. "Said I was trying to 'pull one over' on him! What happened to *your* socks, anyway?"

"I never had time to find any, 'cuz you tried to rat me out to Mom. I had to hurry downstairs to stick up for myself, and then YOU were trying to steal MY bacon!"

"Aww, shuddup. At least you didn't get clobbered on your birthday."

Somehow, that made me feel better. "Yeah, you're right! Happy Birthday, stooge!" I chuckled softly.

Rico's pillow smacked me hard across my exposed right ear. It felt like my eyes were being squeezed out of their sockets. I sat up and looked at him in disbelief.

We both started giggling.

Fight's on, Fight's on!

5
JET SCREAMER

As the youngest of twelve children, I developed a healthy instinct for self preservation very early in life. Being the youngest and smallest, I knew I had no chance of coming out on top if sibling rivalry degenerated into fisticuffs, so any time it looked like pain was coming, I took the next best route: I screamed my fool head off.

Screaming, to my mind, was the simplest and fastest way to end a fight before it ended me. My siblings were more concerned about drawing unwanted parental attention than they were about pounding me, so as soon as I started filling my lungs, they'd usually head for the hills. It wasn't long before this habit earned me a rather derisive sobriquet: Jet Screamer.

If any of my siblings were foolish enough to stick around past the lung-filling stage, they'd be rewarded with a piercing shriek that would grow in intensity from referee's whistle to air raid siren. My lung capacity was such that I could hold a note almost long enough for a parent to arrive on the scene from half a mile away. When they did, I'd be gasping for breath on the floor with my tormentor bent over me, trying desperately to shut me up and looking strangely guilty in the process. I'd avoid getting pounded, the bully would get punished, and I'd usually get off scot-free.

The only time this didn't work was when my parents were away from home. If I had somehow missed their absence, I'd respond to a threat by filling my lungs (instead of the secondary response of running for my life). My tormentor would pause, grin knowingly, and then reward my efforts with punches to the solar plexus, Dutch Rubs to the back of the head, or forcibly flushing my head down the toilet. Getting a swirlie was kryptonite for Jet Screaming - because the last place I wanted to have my mouth wide open was three inches below the surface in the heart of the throne room.

If, on the other hand, my parents were anywhere within earshot of the average steam whistle, Jet Screaming was foolproof. One day, I was burning trash in the 55 gallon oil drum out near our cow pasture. My brother Rico and his malcontent friend Sven were walking down the road next to the pasture, about twenty yards from me. Sven was something of a legend around the neighborhood as the kid who could throw any projectile at any target from any distance - and never miss. The guy made Nolan Ryan looked like a weenie-armed geek.

I had my back to the road, concentrating on getting all the trash into the barrel without lighting the cow pasture on fire. Our cow, Shiner, watched from a distance, hoping I'd produce an apple for him to chew on. As soon as he saw Sven, however, he sidled for cover behind the barn. Cows aren't all that smart, but they're not completely stupid either. I thought nothing of Shiner's sudden disappearance. As I bent over to pick up an armful of newspapers, Sven let fly with a chunk of asphalt he'd pried away from the edge of the road. It whistled through the air and nailed me in the back of the thigh. I dropped like a felled ox.

Rico and Sven roared with laughter. I writhed around in pain, feeling for broken bones in my leg. Then I caught a glimpse of Sven in the corner of my eye, yanking another chunk of asphalt out of the roadbed.

I started filling my lungs.

Rico immediately recognized the signs. "Run!" he told Sven, grabbing at his sleeve.

"What for?" Sven asked. "He's still moving!"

"You don't understand! He's getting ready to…"

The scream started deep in my diaphragm, like a huge turbine engine slowly spinning to life.

"WhhhhhooooooorrrrrRRRRRHHHHH!!"

"C'mon!" Rico shouted.

Sven hefted the chunk of pavement to his shoulder, just as my afterburners kicked in. "RRRRHHHHAAAAHGGGGHH-HGEEEEEEERRRRRHHEEE!!!" Sven's wispy hair flew back from his face and the asphalt was blown from his hand. His glasses fogged up and the loose skin in his cheeks flapped wildly in the storm of my screaming fit. He stumbled backward, fell into the irrigation ditch next to the road, then scrambled out and took off after Rico, who was already disappearing over a distant hill.

I got to my feet, smiling in spite of the welt growing on my leg, and went back to burning trash.

"WHAT'S GOING ON?" My dad's signature bellowed question never failed to strike fear into our hearts. He had an unnerving knack for sneaking up on you when you weren't expecting him. I yelped and almost jumped into the burn barrel, but recovered my wits quickly enough to answer.

"Nothing," I lied. The only danger of Jet Screaming was possibly annoying Dad, who was then likely to punish the first kid he saw, guilty or not.

"Don't tell me 'nothing'!" he shouted. "I heard something!"

"Must have been a jet," I said. "The airport's been pretty busy today."

"That was no jet! I've never heard any jet that sounded like that! Sounded like somebody skinning a cat with a chainsaw! Why, I…" Just then, an Air Force F-4 Phantom roared overhead, lining up on final to the nearby air base. Dad looked up, scrutinizing the jet as it passed. "Sounds like Smitty's got engine problems," he hollered over the noise. "I'd better go have coffee with him and talk it over." Dad would take any excuse to go to the airport restaurant for coffee with his cronies. He was a civilian pilot, but he knew all the Air Force pilots in town too, and couldn't stand not chewing airplane-related fat with any of them. I breathed a sigh of relief as Dad hopped in his car and sped off.

LATER THAT NIGHT, RICO ACCOSTED ME IN OUR BEDROOM AS WE GOT READY for bed. "You little sissy!" he whispered. "You almost got me in trouble with Dad today!"

"I didn't do anything," I said. "You should find smarter friends. Besides, you were three miles away by the time Dad got there!"

"I think you broke Sven's glasses," Rico said, a hint of admiration creeping into his voice. "He said his ears were ringing for an hour!"

"Serves him right," I said. "They're gonna have to repave the road after that clod dug it up trying to kill me."

"Wanna pillow fight?" Rico asked.

"Nah," I said. I'm still out of breath."

A FEW MONTHS LATER, RICO FOUND ME IN OUR ROOM, PLAYING WITH wooden building blocks. I was building a fort, planning to staff it with little plastic army men, then lay siege to it with Rico's teddy bear.

"What are you doing with Harry Beary? Rico demanded. "He's mine!" Before I could give the bear back, Rico had pounced on me. He sat on my chest and pinned my upper arms to the floor with his knees. Then he gleefully started poking me in the chest with staccato jabs from his index fingers.

Poke.

Poke.

Pokity-pokity-pokity-pokity-pokity-poke!

"Gaahhhh!!" I squirmed and writhed with all my strength, but couldn't budge him. Ok, then. Time to fire up the foghorn.

I filled my lungs.

Rico's eyes widened, and he lifted up off my chest, looking like he was heading for the exit. But then an evil grin spread over his face. He suddenly dropped back down, plunking all his weight on my sternum. My lungs emptied like a cheap whoopee cushion, the only sound a pathetic squeak. My tongue lolled out of my mouth.

"Not so fast, Jet Screamer!" He exulted. "All I have to do is make sure you don't breathe, and you can't scream your way to freedom! Go ahead, sissy boy - try to breathe!"

I gasped for air like a fish out of water. But as soon as I'd suck in a lungful, Rico would plunk his weight down on my chest, forcing the air out again.

"That'll teach you to mess with me! You're no match for WEEOOII-WWOWWEEE!!!!"

In a desperate move, I jammed my thumbs as hard as I could up into Rico's armpits. As he dropped down to crush the wind out of me, he unwittingly impaled himself. He recoiled and flopped off of me, rolling around on the floor like his hair was on fire. I slowly climbed to my feet.

"Let that be a lesson to you," I croaked, panting. Then I straightened up and punted Harry Beary right out the door.

No real super-hero has just one super-power. All the good ones always have one last resort to fall back on when their nemesis discovers their kryptonite. Superman has x-ray vision; Batman has a cool car; Spider-man has... umm... ok, he runs around in funny pajamas wearing a mask, so let's forget about him. But me? What's my back-up plan when my gale force shriek springs a slow leak?

I fight dirty.

I may have been rendered powerless by having my life's breath squashed out of me, but my weapon of last resort was simple and effective, and came through in the end.

The saga would continue...

He was born to a dog-eat-dog family...
a mild mannered, tender-hearted runt of the litter...
With no other way to assert himself...
He was forced to accept his destiny - and became...

Jet Screamer!

6

THE BUTCHER

My childhood was spent on a suburban farm of sorts. The older kids had chickens and goats, but by the time I came along, we were down to just the occasional cow, and maybe a horse or two whose owner rented our pasture for the summer. The cows were purchased for the express purpose of providing meat to our small army of hungry mouths. My parents warned us against naming them or forming any attachment to them, because lets face it, it's a lot easier to eat something if you're not accustomed to calling it Pookie.

This warning never went very far with us, though. For whatever reason, we were a sentimental crowd, and as long as any of our animals still had a pulse, we felt compelled to name them and welcome them as another member of our odd clan. But when it came time for butchering, we'd gleefully gather on the pasture fence and watch as the butcher took his rifle and helped our pet to assume room temperature.

Sentimental, yes. Maudlin? No.

ONE OF OUR COWS WAS BLACK WITH A WHITE FACE, WITH A BLACK PATCH around one eye. We affectionately named him Shiner, and spent the better part of a summer getting to know his personality, idiosyncrasies, and overpowering love for munching apples. Shiner spent most of his time bawling out loud for someone to bring him another apple or plotting ways to get the pasture gate open so he could get at the little orchard next to our house and pick them himself. He was a gluttonous cow, with no manners to speak of.

Many mornings that summer broke early with Dad shouting up the stairs at us, "THE COW'S OUT!!" We would respond by leaping out of bed, throwing on our shoes and chasing the idiot bovine from one apple tree to the next all over the neighborhood, until he'd had his fill. Then he'd walk placidly home ahead of us, looking deliberately bored.

Many nights we would camp out in the back yard, and Shiner would bawl urgently at us at the crack of dawn, hoping we'd crawl from our warm sleeping bags and bring him some apples. He kept us awake almost every night, so by the time butchering day came around that fall, our attachment to him had slipped considerably. When the butcher pulled into the driveway that morning, we assumed our places at the fence with morbid satisfaction.

For some reason, my dad had chosen that particular day to be someplace else. He left my sister Emeline in charge, giving her specific instructions for the butchers. They were not, under any circumstance, to drive their truck out into the pasture. It had rained the night before, and since our pasture was already about a half an inch below the normal water table, it would be very easy for a heavy vehicle to sink out of sight in the sodden ground. The butchers arrived, my sister marched up to them as they dismounted their truck, and we watched from the fence with ghoulish anticipation.

"My dad said to tell you not to drive in the pasture," Emeline said confidently. "It's muddy."

The butcher, a self-assured bald man in a filthy cotton t-shirt stretched near the bursting point across a massive belly, smirked at his assistant. "We got four-wheel drive, young lady," he drawled. "We ain't afraid of a little mud!" They both laughed at the very idea that even a *lot* of mud would scare them.

"But Daddy said you'll get stuck if you drive in the pasture!" Emeline said, growing indignant. Indignance is not one of her strong suits, but the idea that she could be held responsible for what might happen next gave her confidence. "It's *really* muddy!"

The butcher snorted. "Ha! Then I'd rather not hafta chase that cow all over the pasture on foot. These are new boots!" He climbed into the cab of the truck and gunned the engine. I couldn't help noticing that his boots looked like he'd pulled them off a shipwreck victim, but that was just one little kid's opinion. Surely this man, this professional, knew what he was talking about? I secretly wished Emeline would stop arguing and open the gate. I'd never seen four-wheel drive in action, and this looked like it might be the day.

Emeline didn't need to open the gate, because the butcher's assistant sauntered over and did it for her, all the time giving her his best 'stand aside, silly girl' look. The butcher cruised through the open gate, and the assistant closed it behind him to make sure Shiner didn't make a break for the apple orchard. The butcher's truck rolled easily across the level field as he stuck his head out the window and shouted happily back at my sister, "Ya see? I don't even need four-wheel dri..."

SCHLUMPF.

The truck suddenly sank to its bumpers, as if it had been driving across a giant bowl of smelly pudding topped by a thin crust of old cow pies. The butcher's smile faded. "Delbert!" he hollered at his assistant. "You, uh, - you come on over and kick in the hubs for me so I can back out, will ya? I don't wanta get my new boots all muddy."

Delbert looked over at my sister, who was smiling evilly.

"Awwww..." he trudged out to the stranded truck, the muddy soil making vile sucking noises at his feet as he went. Shiner stood against the far fence, cocking his head to one side as he tried to figure out if the truck had any apples on board. Delbert dropped to one knee and locked in the hub on the passenger side. When he stood up to go around to the other side, the mud locked his foot in place and he almost fell over trying to get it free. This was getting better by the minute. Delbert wrestled his foot loose, hauled himself around the truck, and locked the other hub.

"Go on," he said, sounding thoroughly disgusted.

The butcher shifted the truck into gear and stomped the gas pedal. Great gobs of mud and cow pie flew from all four tires, a good percentage of it landing on Delbert. The truck didn't budge. The butcher romped on the gas a couple more times and gave up.

"I told you it was muddy!" Emeline said, not even trying to hide the smug satisfaction on her face.

"Give me a push, Delbert," the butcher called from the cab.

Delbert grimaced.

We smiled.

Shiner chewed a rotten apple.

Delbert crouched at the front bumper and put his shoulder against the grill. The butcher stood on the gas again, and Delbert disappeared behind a veil of vile smelling muck. Delbert used a word that we were not supposed to know.

"This ain't gonna work!" Delbert shouted. He tried to storm away from the vehicle, but it's hard to storm convincingly when every step threatens the loss of your boots to a morass of apple-fed bovine effluent. Instead he *shlorped* away gradually. When he finally made it to the fence, he leaned against it, gasping for air.

"You're tearing up the pasture!" Emeline shouted. "Daddy's gonna be ma-ad!" Clearly she was starting to enjoy this.

Frustrated, the butcher stepped out of the truck, only to sink to his knees in the gooey mess. He used the same word that Delbert had. I filed it away in my memory to impress my friends with later. As the butcher struggled to get his new boots loose from the mud, he looked up to see a man in a Jeep parked on the road, watching the scene with benign interest. The Jeep had a large power winch mounted to the front bumper.

The butcher smiled broadly and waved at the Jeep driver, beckoning him. The man got out and walked over to the fence, waiting patiently as the butcher *shlorped* over to him. They seemed to come to some sort of an agreement after several minutes of head shaking, finger pointing and general wild gesticulating. The butcher turned and called to my sister. "You mind if he pulls onto the lawn, so we can hook up the cable and pull our truck out?"

"Don't tear up the grass," Emeline answered with an imperious look. It wasn't as if our lawn was a manicured showpiece; it was mostly brown, and had so many bare spots that it looked more like the back of a giant mangy dog than much of a lawn. All the same, Emeline knew she was making the butcher uncomfortable, so she laid it on thick. "Daddy said you shouldn't tear up the grass. That was right after he said you shouldn't drive in the pasture."

The butcher glared at her, waving the Jeep driver onto the lawn and up to the gate. Delbert struggled over, opened the gate, and started dragging the heavy cable off the winch toward the stranded butcher-mobile. Shiner sidled toward the open gate. He'd run out of apples, and obviously didn't like all the commotion in his pasture.

Delbert jerked up short about twenty feet from the truck. "It ain't long enough!" he shouted in frustration.

"No problem," the Jeep driver said. "I've got four wheel drive!"

We all smiled wider.

Even Shiner grinned a little.

THIRTY SECONDS LATER, THE JEEP WAS BURIED TO ITS BUMPERS TEN FEET behind the truck, and all three men were loudly and rapidly using a lot of words we weren't supposed to know. They were swearing so fast and furious that I couldn't keep track of it all; I considered asking them to repeat themselves so I could memorize it, but I figured they didn't want to be interrupted.

Then a farmer passed by, slowly driving a large tractor down the road. The three men in the pasture froze in mid-cuss; then as one they all started yelling and waving their arms. The farmer glanced over, then stopped his tractor and stared. He saw three mud-encased men standing knee-deep in sludge, next to two four-wheel drive rigs buried in a bog, surrounded by a dozen grubby kids watching from the fence, while one black and white cow tried to act casual as he sidled toward the open gate. The farmer shook his head, immediately doing the mental math and discerning what was going on.

As he wheeled the tractor down onto the lawn, my sister walked over. "I TOLD them not to drive out there, but they wouldn't listen," she explained. The farmer just nodded, smiled and backed the tractor up to the gate. He stood up on the seat and directed the three men to hook the winch cable to the butcher's truck. Then he dug in a tool box behind the seat and produced a heavy canvas tow strap, which he hurled out into the mud. It landed with a splash that splattered the butcher's greasy t-shirt. The farmer watched patiently as the butcher connected the strap to the rear of the Jeep, then slogged back and connected the other end to the tow hook on the tractor.

"You boys get in them rigs and put 'em in neutral," the farmer ordered.

"Just get us moving," the Jeep driver offered. "We can use four-wheel drive to get the rest of the way."

"Four-wheel drive got you into this mess," the farmer said patiently. "It ain't gonna get you out. Just put 'em in neutral and steer."

The Jeep driver hung his head in shame.

When all three vehicles were connected, the farmer slipped the tractor into low gear and crept forward. The tow strap drew tight and twanged like a bowstring, and the Jeep shuddered - but didn't budge. The farmer eased into the throttle, careful to keep his huge drive wheels from breaking traction. All eyes focused on the tractor, waiting for the big tires to start tearing up the lawn.

Shiner sidled closer to the gate.

Thinking quickly, my brother Rico hurled a rotten apple past Shiner's head. The cow instantly forgot what he was doing and trotted after it. He picked it up out of the mud and contentedly smacked his lips around it. He was careful to lick his lips when it was gone, to be sure he hadn't missed a scrap. I don't know why he felt compelled to lick the inside of his nostrils as well, but there's no understanding cows.

Meanwhile, the tractor was beginning to dig ruts in our yard, but the stranded trucks were breaking free at last. Delbert, stumbling along beside the butcher's truck in an attempt to supervise, tripped and fell flat. He planted one outstretched hand dead center in a fresh cow pie, and immediately shouted out what seemed to me to be the new word of the day. I *really* couldn't wait to use that word on my friends.

Delbert dragged himself to his feet, flicking his hand rapidly in an attempt to get the freshest part of the cow pie off. "Dirty son-of-a..." he stopped short as he realized I was now hanging on his every word.

Son of a WHAT, Delbert? Son of a WHAT??!?? I thought, almost unable to bear it. The other word they'd all been throwing around was great, but the suspense of this curse left unfinished was making my young brain work overtime with the possibilities. I momentarily toyed with the idea of becoming a butcher someday, just so I could learn the last word in the phrase.

Delbert wiped his hand on his muddy jeans and slogged ahead.

The farmer had found the sweet spot between throttle and clutch, and was now dragging the marooned vehicles free. The big tractor tires had done a number on our lawn in the process, though. Emeline was looking nervously at the deep ruts in the grass, knowing Dad would come home and be eager to blame somebody. As the butcher's truck finally cleared the gate, she kept muttering to herself, "Daddy's gonna be ma-ad..."

Talk about stating the obvious, I thought. No point worrying about what he'll say, when you *know* it's gonna be bad. I figured it would be better to focus on the spectacle at hand, and worry about the consequences later. I didn't want to waste perfectly good entertainment by worrying about who'd get the blame for it. Besides, now that the trucks were unstuck, the butcher would be getting his rifle out!

———

THE FARMER SHOOK HANDS WITH THE BUTCHER AND THE JEEP DRIVER, accepting their thanks and waving off their half-hearted offers of cash payment. He stowed his tow strap and climbed back aboard his tractor. "You tell your daddy I'm sorry about the lawn," he said in a kindly tone to Emeline. "Couldn't be helped. You have him come talk to me if he has any questions."

The farmer grew immensely in all our estimation at that point, because offering to answer Dad's inevitable questioning was like offering yourself up to be interrogated by the Gestapo during World War II. The guy looked like a hero to me as he drove off, and I toyed with the idea of becoming a farmer.

The butcher's grumbling nearby shook me out of my reverie. He was resting his rifle on the top rail of the fence, hoping Shiner would present an easy shot. "Hold still, you dirty son-of-a..."

Son of a WHAT??? I thought frantically. Somebody please tell me!

Shiner held still for a moment, but just as the butcher squeezed the trigger, he jumped forward for no apparent reason. The bullet hit him in the leg, which seemed to annoy him more than anything. The butcher was using a .22 caliber rifle, which would only be deadly with a perfectly placed shot to the brain. Any place else on a full grown cow would probably feel like a really nasty horsefly. Shiner trotted away, eyeballing the butcher nervously.

"Whyn't you let me do it?" Delbert asked in a patronizing tone. "I'm a better shot, anyway."

"Pipe down," the butcher grumbled, taking aim again. The rifle cracked, and the bullet ricocheted away with a harmless *twang*. Shiner looked annoyed, but showed no sign of being hit.

"Ya missed 'im clean that time!" Delbert crowed. "Let me try." The butcher glared at Delbert, but handed over the rifle. "Ya gotta breathe out before you pull the trigger," Delbert said. "Watch this." He raised the rifle to his shoulder and fired, barely bothering to aim. Shiner bellowed and dropped in the mud, instantly laying still.

"Ya see what I mean?" Delbert was grinning. "All it takes is a steady hand..."

Shiner stood up.

"Nice shot," the butcher scoffed. "You and your steady hand almost gave him a heart attack."

I was beginning to think that if these two idiots were any indication, being a butcher was not the career for me.

"Awww, son-of-a..." Delbert whined.

SONOFA WHAT, DELBERT???? SONOFA WHAAAATTT!?!?!?!???

"We could just get him to come over here." Everybody turned at once. My brother Jethro was holding an apple in one hand, dangling it over the fence. Shiner was already weighing the pros and cons of coming closer to the rifle in order to get the apple.

Apple? Gunfire. Gunfire? Apple!

The butcher frowned. "That stupid cow ain't coming over here after he's been shot three times!"

"Twice," Delbert corrected. "You missed once."

"Shaddap," the butcher said. "It don't matter anyway, 'cause like I said..."

Shiner started trotting toward Jethro's apple, his eyes glazed with gluttony.

———

SEVERAL DAYS LATER, WE PICKED UP WHAT WAS LEFT OF SHINER FROM THE butcher shop. He returned home one final time, neatly packaged in white waxed paper with the specific cuts clearly labeled on the outside. Jethro and my brother Inigo thoughtfully re-labelled each package before loading them in the freezer, so that 'Rump Roast' now read, 'Shiner's Rump Roast,' and 'Burger' now read 'R.I.P. Shiner Burger.' My sisters collectively described this act as 'gross', 'cruel' and 'morbid', but we boys all thought it was a fitting tribute. Shiner was gone, but his memory lived on.

Dad groused about the destroyed yard and the huge ruts in the pasture for weeks after the incident, but none of us actually got in trouble for it - thanks largely to the farmer's offer to throw himself on his sword. If he'd known the explosive nature of Dad's temper, he may not have been so magnanimous - but we weren't complaining. The pasture was sold off and subdivided years later, but the scars from the ruts in the yard remained for decades. Grass stubbornly refused to grow on the spot, and I often thought that was Shiner's final revenge for being lured to his doom by the disingenuous offer of his favorite treat.

I was only five or six years old at the time, so my recollection is probably less than complete, but it does seem to me that Shiner was the last of our cows. After that, we gave up raising our own beef and resorted to buying it like normal people.

And beef has never been quite the same...

7

YELLOW JACKET, WHERE IS THY STING?

THE GREAT OUTDOORS IS A PLACE FULL OF WONDER AND BEAUTY, sometimes livened up by danger and discomfort. I always feel in awe when I'm in the woods, sitting by a clear mountain lake or watching an eagle soar. These moments help me to appreciate the pure majesty of God's creation, and I'm never in any hurry to return to civilization.

Then I get stung by a yellow jacket.

This always brings my reverie to a screeching, painful halt. The screeching is intended to strike the offending insect dead by the sheer force of its delivery, and hopefully prevent further doses of pain. What is it about me that yellow jackets, wasps, hornets, honey bees, and most other aggressive insects with pointy parts find impossible to resist? I attract the vermin from out of nowhere, for no apparent reason - maybe I'm just an easy target.

I wasn't always such a desirable victim. When I was a child, I ignored bees and they ignored me. We had something of a gentleman's agreement: I leave you alone, and you don't sting me. You don't sting me, and I won't squash you like the annoying little bug that you are. But over the past several decades, members of the bee world have for some reason decided to violate our unspoken treaty. When I go into the woods these days, it's like I have a price on my head, and every bee under the sun is trying to poke me to death in order to collect the bounty. This annoying trend started one year when I took a summer job on a land surveying crew with the U.S. Forest Service. Until then, I had only been stung twice in my life, and both were justifiable cases of mistaken identity.

THE FIRST INCIDENT HAPPENED WHEN I WAS NINE. MY FRIEND RICHIE AND I were walking down the bank of an irrigation canal that ran behind his house, on our way to work on the cave we had been digging all summer. We hadn't decided what to do with the cave when we finished it, but when you're a nine year old boy with a shovel, the world is your oyster, and large holes in the ground have ways of finding entertaining uses all by themselves. We were happily kicking the heads off of dandelions and chopping weeds with our shovels as we walked, pretending to be brave swordsmen lopping the heads off of marauding barbarians.

"Watch this," Richie said, raising his shovel over his head to deliver the coup de grace to another barbarian weed.

I have since learned to recognize the phrase "Watch this" as a reason for concern, if not an outright harbinger of disaster. Richie drove the point of his shovel through the stalk of the brittle dead weed, causing it to collapse and uproot itself from the loose soil. Unfortunately, a horde of barbarian yellow jackets had chosen the root of that very weed as the roof of their nest, and didn't appreciate it being abruptly opened like a pop top soda can.

I watched in morbid fascination as the angry insects swarmed out into the sunlight, looking for the guilty home wrecker. I was only a few feet away, feeling like a silent witness to a crime. Richie, with his shovel still in hand, was the obvious prime suspect. The swarm descended on him like the crack of doom. Stunned, he looked out at me from the center of a swirling yellow and black cloud.

"BEEEEEEEEES!!!!!!!!"

No, I thought. *Technically, those are yellow jackets. They're hornets, not bees.*

I would have corrected Richie's amateurish misidentification of the species, but he was off like a shot, his shovel twirling in midair above where he had been standing. I turned to go with him, partly to make sure that he got home all right, but mostly to see if he ended up with any cool scars. As I tensed to make my exit, I felt a sharp pain in my thigh and noticed a lone yellow jacket happily stinging my leg.

Without so much as a yelp, I acted instinctively and squashed the little bugger with the palm of my hand. He no doubt had mistaken me for Richie, and attacked in the heat of the moment. Understandable, but not quite enough for me to allow him to make the same mistake twice. Remember the gentleman's agreement: You get stung, you get to squish.

No hard feelings, that's just the way the game is played.

Richie made it home alive, where his screaming entry through the back door caused his mother to age prematurely and jump up and down at a high rate of speed. His older brother calmly slapped the remaining yellow jackets to death, all the while telling Richie what a big crybaby he was. Seeing his brother's cool composure, I resolved that I would never be a crybaby in the face of a little pain, especially pain inflicted by animals roughly the size and intelligence of the average kidney bean.

From that day on, I planned to regard all stinging members of the insect world with little or no interest. This philosophy served me well for the remainder of my childhood, with one exception.

ONE SUMMER SEVERAL YEARS LATER, I WAS VACATIONING AT A LAKE retreat with some friends, lounging on the dock and soaking up sun between cannonball contests. Suddenly, a large and rather loud bumblebee made an unprovoked high speed pass right in front of my nose. I ignored it, as was by now my practice, writing it off as a navigational error on the part of the bee. Had he continued on his way, I would have forgotten about it and got right back to working on my sunburn, but the bee had other plans.

After passing within an inch of my nose, he added power, pulled into a steep climbing turn, and came back for another run. This time he missed by half the distance of the first pass, and immediately maneuvered for another. I knew I had done nothing wrong, so I decided the bee was quite insane. He was either bent on committing suicide by rearranging my nose, or was intent on putting my eye out just for the fun of it. I jumped up, striking a pose like King Kong preparing to swat biplanes from atop the Empire State building.

Too bad for me. We all know how that one turned out.

The bee continued to swoop and dive at my head, while I backed up and swatted wildly at the empty air behind him. Boat docks are not an ideal place for this type of activity, since they are generally narrow and leave little room for error when one is stumbling backward in a blind panic. This dock was no exception, and it wasn't long before I found myself teetering on its brink, struggling to maintain my balance while keeping my guard up. Seeing my predicament, the bee aimed directly between my eyes and lit the afterburners.

In the end, I got to go swimming once more than I'd bargained for, and the bee got to go back to the hive and laugh it up with his friends at my expense. The incident struck me as a random act of senseless violence, not enough to make me abandon the gentlemen's agreement. I still regarded most stinging insects as benign, and this particular sociopath as nothing more than a rare exception to the rule.

THE SECOND STINGING OF MY PRE-FOREST SERVICE DAYS OCCURRED AFTER I was grown and had succumbed to my inner renegade by purchasing a motorcycle. I loved the feeling of freedom the bike gave me as I cruised along, weaving through traffic jams and accelerating around slow-pokes and lost picnickers.

As I was riding home from work one day, something struck me in the chest just above the top button of my shirt. I glanced around, but couldn't find what hit me. I assumed it was any one of a million types of harmless flying bugs that decorate the fronts of motor vehicles world wide, so I forgot about it.

When I got home, I parked my bike and went inside. As I twisted around to close the front door behind me, something started stabbing me repeatedly just above the small of my back. I leapt up and down and twirled around in circles, trying desperately to reach the spot. My cat watched with mild concern from across the room, muscles tensed for a quick exit in case I got too close. After a few seconds of ineffectual thrashing, I flopped down on the floor and rolled around like I was on fire. The stabbing abruptly stopped.

The episode had a simple explanation. As I rode home, a yellow jacket had unwittingly flown into my path and struck me in the chest, the impact knocking him momentarily senseless. He fell inside the front of my shirt, and awoke minutes later to find himself trapped in a strange place, going who knows where. He shook himself off and got up to go looking for a way out.

I didn't feel him wandering around because I was wearing a t-shirt under my work shirt, and he was sandwiched between the two layers. By the time I made it home, he had made his way around my back, to the exact spot that is humanly impossible to reach without detaching your arms. When I turned to close the door, my shirt stretched tight over the yellow jacket, making him think that someone was trying to squish him - which wasn't exactly true until a second later. He responded by stinging as fast as his stinger could sting, and I responded by flailing as fast as my flailers could flail.

Once again: You get squished, you get to sting, and if you get stung, you get to squish. Both of us reacted to the situation as per the gentleman's agreement, and I had no hard feelings toward the bug for thinking my shirt was a mortal threat.

But I still had to kill him.

THE ABOVE INCIDENTS NOTWITHSTANDING, MY PHILOSOPHY REGARDING bees and their ilk remained basically the same. Peaceful coexistence was the way for me. That's why I was confused when I was viciously attacked by hornets during my first summer with the Forest Service. I was surveying a wilderness boundary along the side of a mountain, minding my own business, when suddenly the air was filled with the angry buzz of a swarm of hornets. Thinking the gentleman's agreement was still in effect, I trotted back the way I had come, planning to let them vent their collective spleens at a safe distance before continuing my job.

Suddenly, I felt a stab on the back of my hand. Before I could slap in reply, the hornet had stung me twice more, right through the back of my glove. I slapped him dead, and was promptly greeted by the rest of the swarm rushing to his defense. I bolted off down the mountain, surrendering nearly ten thousand dollars worth of surveying equipment to a swarm of insects. Surprising how fast pain changes your priorities. I figured my equipment would be safe with them, since they couldn't carry it and wouldn't know what to do with it if they could. Besides, any prospective human thieves would most likely get the same surly reception I had.

After outrunning the hornets, I tried to remove my glove to assess the damage. To my shock, my hand was swelling up so fast that I almost couldn't get the glove off. When I finally did yank it free, my hand looked like a rubber surgical glove inflated to about 75 PSI. I couldn't bend my fingers, and my entire hand ached. I had never had any reaction to stings in the past. For some reason, the bee world had upped the ante: They were using poison!

That did it for me.

The war was on.

I would no longer meekly give a hive or nest a wide berth in the interest of diplomacy and détente, oh no. Now I would go out of my way to destroy, kill, harass, and otherwise annoy any bee or related insect, whether they stung first or not.

As that summer passed and the next one arrived, I found myself back at the Forest Service, the undisputed winner of the Most Stings award from the previous year. Forest Service employees see this as something of a medal of honor – whoever got stung the most was the one doing the most work. This is not necessarily true – I watched one of my co-workers get stung while he was sleeping during his lunch break – but nonetheless, the competition was always closely watched and highly regarded by all.

In one instance, I suffered dual stings from a pair of yellow jackets, simultaneously delivered to identical spots on each of my forearms as I was frantically crashing through a thicket in a vain attempt to escape. The attack was, I must say, a masterpiece of coordination and timing on the part of the yellow jackets. One of them even got away, because just as I was about to slap him flat, I was clotheslined by a low hanging branch, giving him the diversion he needed to beat a hasty retreat. His partner was not as lucky - I'd angrily pancaked him a split second earlier.

When I regained consciousness, my forearms had swollen to Popeye-like proportions, and the impact with the branch had tattooed my neck with bark and sap. A few inches higher, and I'd have resembled Popeye more than I would have liked. Luckily for me, I came out of it with both eyes intact, albeit somewhat reddened by fury.

Several days later, we were surveying a steep wooded area for a future logging road. Our duties included measuring and marking the distance along the proposed route. This was done by dragging a long tape measure called a "chain" through the woods and placing stakes at one hundred foot intervals. I was at the back end of the chain, while my crew chief was in the lead, setting the pace by tugging gently on the chain. It was fairly mind numbing work, and I eventually fell into a sort of barely conscious, walking boredom. Then I noticed that the tugging from the front of the chain had stopped.

I looked up to see my boss flinching and ducking like he was being stuck with a hot poker. From a hundred feet back, I couldn't see what was bothering him, but I *knew*. His eyes darted back and forth, tracking some flying insect that I couldn't quite make out. I could tell it was closing in as my boss started wildly swinging his hands ever closer to his face. He was getting more desperate by the swing, and the breaking point came when he inadvertently slapped his own glasses off his head, sending them pirouetting off through the trees. Now defenseless *and* blind, he decided to retreat.

Watching someone trying to escape a bee attack can be entertaining all by itself, but when the attack occurs in the woods, the combination of thick underbrush, rocks, and treacherous terrain make any retreat an exercise in agility and luck. The fact that my boss couldn't see more than two feet without his glasses made it even more entertaining. I was still laughing three hours later as we were driving back into town. The only time I appreciate bees is when they're stinging somebody else.

LATER THAT SUMMER, THE FOREST SERVICE DECIDED THAT THE LARGE number of bee stings suffered by crews in the woods called for preventive measures. We were forced to take a first aid class to learn how to treat bee stings in the field. Apparently, bee venom can be dangerous when administered to the right person in a large enough dose, and the Forest Service didn't want to have to write any letters to our families, explaining how we had given our lives in the valiant construction of skid trails and drainage ditches. Part of our training involved learning how to properly inject a sting victim with anti-venom in the event of a severe allergic reaction.

Under normal conditions, I am not one who gets queasy at the thought of being poked by a needle. But when our instructor informed us that in order to graduate the course we would have to actually stick needles into each other, I balked. I can sit there all day long while doctors and nurses poke me full of holes like a human pincushion, but the idea of being on the other side of the syringe just didn't appeal to me. It was bad enough that the bees of the world were aggressively poking us every chance they got, but now they had us poking each other, too. I probably would have failed the course, but my boss, who also happened to be my shot partner, cured my reluctance with one word.

"Sissy."

I took a small amount of sadistic pleasure in stabbing him. Suddenly, I saw things from the yellow jackets' point of view. Stinging some bungling idiot for squishing your cousins or wrecking your house may not exactly even the score - but it sure *feels* good.

8

LIKE A BLIND COW...

"MAN, IT'S RAININ' LIKE A BLIND COW PEEIN' ON A FLAT ROCK!" MOJO shook his hat off, spraying water everywhere.

"Why's the cow gotta be blind?" I asked.

"Huh?"

"The cow," I said. "What difference does it make if the cow's blind? It'll make the same amount of mess if it pees on a flat rock whether it's blind or not, right?"

"You Yankees are always askin' silly questions," Mojo said, disgusted.

Mojo was a man of many one-liners - all of them odd.

Mojo was my roommate for much of the time I served in the U.S. Air Force. We were both small town boys, but because he was from a little town in East Texas and I was from a little town in Southern Oregon, many of his one-liners didn't immediately translate. I'd always laugh at his sayings, but I usually couldn't stand to not ask what the devil he was talking about. Who knew that Redneckish could have so many different dialects?

Once we went to the chow hall together to have dinner. As we came to the end of the buffet line, Mojo exclaimed in a happy voice, "Awww, they got poot-root pie, boy! Gonna get me some poot-root pie!" He was grinning like a fool.

I looked around. There were several varieties of pie at the end of the display case; apple, lemon meringue, pumpkin. I had no idea what he was going on about, and said so.

"You mean you ain't never had no poot-root pie?!? You damn Yankees don't know what yer missin'!" He grabbed a dish with a slice of pumpkin pie on it. "You better get you some, boy," he warned me.

"Should I even bother to ask?"

"Ask what?"

"Why you call pumpkin pie 'poot-root'."

"Man," he said, as if he were talking to a really dense four year old. "This ain't no punkin! Them's sweet potatoes!" He thrust the pie under my nose. "Can't you tell the difference?"

"Er, no. Does it taste like pumpkin?"

"Naw, man! It's way better! You better get you some!"

I was VERY dubious, since I hate sweet potatoes almost as much as I hate brussels sprouts - which I flatly refuse to eat based solely on their repulsive odor. Sweet potatoes are only slightly less vile. "I'll try it," I said, reluctantly taking a slice from the case, "but if it tastes like a cow pie, I'm gonna make you eat the rest of it."

"Fine by me," Mojo said. "Silly Yankee can't even appreciate a good poot-root pie, my Lord…" He walked off, muttering in disgust.

When we got to our table, I took a tiny bite of my pie. It tasted exactly like pumpkin.

"Tastes like pumpkin to me," I said.

Mojo glared at me. "That's 'cuz you got no taste. Any fool can tell that's poot-root."

"All right," I said, giving in. "Why 'poot root'?"

Mojo broke into his classic 'I'm fixin' to laugh at my own joke' grin. "'Cuz you eat too much of it, it'll make you poot!" He laughed out loud until he had tears in his eyes. "Oh, Lord, that's funny!" I stared at him for a moment, then smiled and ate my pumpkin - er - *poot-root* pie. I didn't really care what was in it, as long as it tasted like pumpkin.

After dinner, we headed back toward our dorm. Mojo stretched his arms over his head as we walked, then absently scratched his belly.

"That was some good, boy," he said. "And now, I think I best go back to the house and scrub some bugs."

I looked at him. "Do *what*?" This was how many of our conversations went.

"Scrub some bugs, man!" He looked at me, obviously exasperated. "Offa my backside, get it?"

"You got bugs on your backside, Mojo, I don't want to know about it. And whose house are you talking about? We live in a closet that doubles as a dorm room."

"Naw, man - I mean I'm fixin' to take a shower! And anyplace I hang my hat is my house, ya silly Yankee!" He walked off toward our dorm building. I followed, smiling. Mojo was good company, even if he was impossible to understand.

WE WERE BOTH AIR TRAFFIC CONTROLLERS, BUT MOJO WORKED IN THE control tower, and I worked in the RAPCON, or Radar Approach Control. My workplace was a dark room with a bunch of green tinted radar scopes, while Mojo worked in a room with a view. We had the same shifts, so we'd often hear each other on the inter-facility phone when one of us needed to coordinate flight information. The phone line and all the radio frequencies in both facilities were always recorded, so that if anything went wrong, the investigators could figure out who to blame.

One quiet summer evening, the line buzzed at my scope. There was no traffic to speak of, since the local fighter wing was done flying for the day. I selected the line to stop it ringing. "Recorded line, Airman MacDougall."

"Hey MP!" Mojo's voice was almost a whisper. "You gotta get me outta here, man!"

"What are you talking about?"

"He's doing it again, man!" Mojo whispered, a touch of revulsion creeping into his voice.

"Who's doing what? Will you get to the point? I'm working here!"

"Don't lie, man. I know you trolls are sitting' down there playin'

Spades and drinking coffee. I bet you haven't talked to a single plane in the last two hours."

"You do realize this is a recorded line, right?"

"Yeah. So? I'm just giving you something to record, 'cuz I know you're not workin' planes."

"I didn't say I was working *planes*." I paused to collect the last trick in the hand, flashing a triumphant grin at the three other controllers I was playing Spades with. "I *am* working on embarrassing a couple of rubes, though, so quit distracting me. What do you want?" The other card players gave up and headed for the coffee pot in the break room.

"It's Sergeant Grohpe, man. He's at it again." Sergeant Burton Grohpe was Mojo's supervisor. He wasn't exactly right in the head and didn't mind demonstrating it. Mojo was alone in the tower cab with him.

"What's he doing this time?"

"Tai Chi."

"Say again?"

"He's doing Tai Chi," Mojo said. "Standing on the console in front of the windows."

"O-K. That's not so bad," I said. Tai Chi is pretty harmless, and Grohpe was capable of much worse.

"He's facing the sunset, doing Tai Chi," Mojo paused to shudder audibly. Then he whispered, "In a *Speedo*."

"Ewww," I said. "That's just not right!" Sergeant Grohpe was not exactly what you'd call a chiseled example of the adult male anatomy. The resulting mental picture was disturbing.

"Tell *me* about it," Mojo hissed. "He looks like a fat, bald Karate Kid. Only he's wearing a Speedo. And combat boots. And his headset. You gotta get me outta here, man!"

"What do ya want me to do? I'm not the boss of you! Wait a minute - he's wearing his headset? What's he got it clipped to?" Our headsets had clips on the handset portion that you could attach to your belt, as well as little alligator clips on the cord, so you could clip it to your collar and keep it from tangling around your coffee cup. "Wait, no - don't tell me!"

Mojo ignored me. "He's got the handset clipped to the waistband of his Speedo,"

"Stop! I don't wanta know!"

"and the cord is clipped to his chest somewhere…"

"Aagghh! Stop! You're gonna make me hurl!"

"…I think it's either tangled in his chest hair, or it's clipped to a nipple. I didn't want to look too close."

"Ecch! I'm gonna have nightmares about this!"

"Maybe you could call the Flight Surgeon's office. They might come and haul him off in a rubber truck!"

"I doubt that. The most they ever do is tell you to take some Tylenol. I swear - I nearly broke my ankle playing basketball last week, so I went to the Flight Doc. Know what he did?"

"Emergency lobotomy?"

"No, smart guy. He gave me Tylenol. I coulda done that myself. I had to crawl back to my truck to get home."

"So what's your point?"

"My point is that the most the Flight Doc is gonna do to Grohpe is give him some Tylenol and a pat on the head and send him back to work. Where he'll be writing *your* annual performance evaluation. Probably still in his Speedo."

"Isshh," Mojo sounded like he'd just caught a whiff of skunk. "What should I do, then? I swear, if he starts doing Downward Facing Dog, I'm gonna jump offa the catwalk!"

"You could always join him," I cracked. "Might get you a better evaluation!"

"You're sick, man. Besides, I don't wear no Speedos."

"You're probably right," I said. "You doing Tai Chi in your tighty-whities is almost as bad as Grohpe doing it in his banana hammock."

"Aww, man - now you're gonna make me hurl!"

"You better pray Grohpe didn't have poot-root pie for dinner - I'll hafta call the coroner for you instead of the rubber truck for him."

"Cut it out, man! You'll ruin me for poot-root pie for the rest of my life!"

"Sorry. Tell ya what - there's not gonna be any more traffic all night. Just ask Grohpe if you can leave early. He won't care - it'll give him a chance to Face his Downward Dog in peace. I'll try to get out of here too, and we can go catfishing."

"Okay," Mojo said with relief. "Anything's better than watching this. But I gotta warn ya - there's some thunderstorms building up. You better not mind gettin' wet, 'cuz by the time we get out to the river, its gonna be rainin' like a..."

"I know, I know," I interrupted. "Like a blind cow..."

9

TRAVELS WITH CHUMLEY

DOGS ARE A NECESSARY INGREDIENT FOR ALMOST ANY SUCCESSFUL outdoor adventure. They get into trouble, bark at random noises, roll in dead things when you least expect it, and generally up the entertainment value of any trip without much effort required on your part. Although I am an avowed cat person, I readily admit the utility and value of a good dog on a camping or hunting trip - cats just can't be bothered to retrieve ducks or chase The Foot away from your tent when you really need them to.

My brother Jethro had a Newfoundland named Chumley who was fantastic at raising the entertainment level wherever he went. At 165 lbs, Chumley was a giant among dogs, even if he was a teddy bear at heart. It was not unusual to find Chumley sleeping on Jethro's back porch in the dead of winter, with three cats curled up asleep on top of him. He loved everybody and everything, and wouldn't have hurt a fly even if it had spent all day plucking individual hairs out of his massive nose.

Jethro would often go out of town on vacation and leave Chumley with me. I enjoyed taking care of him, since it allowed me to test drive a dog without having to buy his food, and I got a kick out of how people would react to him. His sheer size was often a conversation starter. Once when I was taking Chumley for a walk near my home, an elderly gentleman eased his car up next to me.

"Is - is that a BEAR??" he asked, voice quavering.

I looked at him, then pointedly looked at Chumley's long tail. "Noo," I said. "It's a dog."

"Well, what on earth do you feed a dog that size?"

I couldn't resist. "Bears," I said. "He really likes bears." The man's eyes bugged out as Chumley panted and drooled on himself, his tongue the size and shape of a slobbery pink doormat.

"Well, ok, then!" the man said. As he drove off I could see him staring in his rear view mirror in disbelief.

"Good boy, Chumley," I said.

ON ANOTHER VISIT, CHUMLEY WAS SLEEPING IN THE BACK OF MY PICKUP AS we drove across town to visit my brother Rico. A teenage girl was following us too closely and rear-ended my pickup as she tried to send a text message.

"Son of a..." I muttered as I pulled to the side of the road. I walked around to the back of the truck to inspect the damage. Two of the four bolts holding the step bumper to the pickup frame had sheared off, allowing the bumper to swing on the remaining two bolts like a hinge. It dangled under the bed, but there was no other damage to either vehicle.

The girl got out of her car and joined me behind my truck. "OH MY GOSH!" she gasped. "Are you ok?"

"Yeah, I'm.."

"OH NO! I broke your truck!! My parents are going to kill me! Are you ok?"

"Yeah, it's no prob.."

"My parents are going to kill me! They're out of town and this is my mom's car and I'm not supposed to drive it, and OH MY GOSH! Is it ruined?"

"It's fine. I can fix..."

"It looks ruined! Can you fix it? OH MY GOSH!"

I gave up trying to get a word in and just let her prattle on. Eventually she ran out of breath and had to pause. At that moment, Chumley woke up. He had slept through the entire thing, and now he lumbered to his feet. The girl was standing with her back to my truck, looking at a tiny blemish on her front bumper. Chumley stuck his head over the tailgate and peered over her shoulder, trying to see what she was looking at. Then he sighed in her ear.

"AAAAAH!" she squealed, almost jumping into traffic. "IS HE GOING TO EAT ME?!?"

Good Boy, Chumley.

ANOTHER TIME, I TOOK HIM FOR A HIKE TO A MOUNTAIN LAKE. THE LAKE was set at the end of a small meadow, about twenty yards from where the trail left the tree line. I was several yards behind Chumley when he caught scent of the water, and because he was a water dog and it was a hundred degrees outside, he naturally broke into a run. He hit the water like a battleship coming out of dry dock and immediately began loudly splashing and slurping, sending spray everywhere. As I came out of the tree line behind him, I noticed a young lady sitting on a blanket about thirty yards further up the shore from where Chumley was wallowing. She and Chumley noticed each other at that same moment.

Before I could say 'dumb dog', Chumley had bolted from the water and made a beeline for the lady's blanket. His tongue was flapping in the breeze behind him, and he was scattering water and mud everywhere. The young lady drew in a sharp breath and froze as Chumley thrust his massive toothy mug in her face - then he shook himself off vigorously.

"EEEEEEP!" she squealed.

"Good boy, Chumley," I thought.

JET SCREAMER

ONE OF CHUMLEY'S FINEST MOMENTS HAPPENED ON ANOTHER backpacking trip, where my brothers and I set up camp next to a pristine mountain lake. The campsite was on an unbelievably picturesque grassy meadow, with the lake at one end and a stunning view of a mountain beyond. It was idyllic. After we made it to camp, I decided to rest my feet and take a nap before rousting up something for dinner. Rico and Jethro set about making their dinners while I dozed.

Rico's favorite camp dinner is hot dogs. He takes great care to pack all the necessary condiments into tiny containers, and he looks forward with great expectations to that first dog coming off the fire. There was a downed log along one edge of our campsite that made a perfect prep area, and Rico had carefully spread out all his supplies on it.

He was meticulously assembling the various parts - bun, cheese, dog, mustard, relish, catsup, etc., but he wasn't alone. Chumley had given up his search for dead animals to roll in and caught a whiff of Rico's food. He sidled up behind Rico, massive black head hovering just behind Rico's left hip. I watched from under the brim of my hat.

This could get good.

Meanwhile, Jethro was struggling to get his camp stove to keep an even flame without lighting his shirt on fire. He was making a pot full of instant macaroni and cheese - probably because Chumley ate all of his deviled eggs on the way to the trailhead.

As Jethro stirred his toxic cheese, Rico put the finishing touches on his hot dog. He picked it up in his right hand and turned to his left to find a place to sit. As he turned, Chumley held perfectly still - except his mouth, which he opened wider than a feeding hippo. Rico completed his turn and unwittingly shoved his dinner straight into the dog's mouth. Chumley clamped his jaw shut and held tight.

"Hey!" Rico said, tugging on the hot dog. "HEY!!" he gave the hot dog a vicious yank, breaking off most of it in Chumley's mouth. Rico stared at the remaining morsel in his hand in disbelief. Chumley swallowed once, not bothering with chewing.

"YOU STUPID SON OF A...!" Rico shouted. He threw the last bit of hot dog at Chumley, trying to assert some shred of dominance. Chumley's mouth snapped open and shut, his body never moving.

The hot dog was gone. "GAAAAH!" Rico screamed. Jethro and I burst out laughing as Chumley looked around for the second course.

"Good boy, Chumley," Jethro and I said.

"BAD BOY, CHUMLEY!" Rico hollered.

I laid back down, chuckling. As I drifted off, Jethro muttered something about going down to the lake for more water. He took his pot of nasty pasta off the stove and set it on a log.

Moments later, I woke to Jethro shouting.

"Hey, Hey, HEYYY!!"

I sat up. Chumley was standing over the pot of mac and cheese, his face buried up to his ears. He looked up at Jethro. There was a single piece of macaroni stuck to the end of his snout.

"YOU STUPID SON OF A...!" Jethro shouted.

"Good Boy Chumley," I said.

"BAD BOY, CHUMLEY!" Jethro and Rico hollered in stereo.

Chumley licked his lips.

"Ya dope!" Jethro grabbed the pot and turned on me. "I told ya to watch my food!"

"What are you talking about?" I asked. "All I heard was you were going to get more water. Besides, mac and cheese isn't really food, anyway. Unless you're ten years old. Or a dog."

Jethro looked at Chumley. "Ya stoop!" he swung a half-hearted kick at the dog's backside. Chumley took that as a cue for play time, jumped out of the way and started tearing wildly around the camp site, knocking over random equipment, piled firewood, Rico's tent and Jethro's coffee pot.

"Good Boy, Chumley," I said.

"BAD BOY, CHUMLEY!!" Jethro swung a more serious kick, but Chumley easily dodged it. Jethro almost fell on his backside.

"Good Boy, Chumley!"

"You shaddap!" Jethro growled. "You're just encouraging him!"

"What's your point?"

Chumley gave up on the game of chase and crawled into Jethro's tent, rolling around happily on his sleeping bag.

"GAAAH!!" Jethro hollered. "Get offa my sleeping bag, ya lummox!"

"Good Boy, Chumley!" Rico said.

"Morons," Jethro muttered. He looked down at his hand, noticing for the first time that he was still holding the half-empty pot of mac and cheese.

"Looks like you're skipping dinner," I chuckled.

Jethro looked into the pot. He paused for a breath, then shrugged. He whipped his spoon out of his back pocket and took a bite.

Rico and I fought back our gag reflexes. Chumley stopped rolling in Jethro's sleeping bag and perked up his ears, ready to catch any crumbs.

"Oh man, you're sick!" Rico looked liked he'd just bit a lemon. "You're gonna get food poisoning!"

"Pssshhh," Jethro scoffed. "It's just a little dog slobber. It doesn't hurt him, does it?" Chumley smiled and wagged his tail.

"I think I'm glad he ate my hot dog, 'cuz if he hadn't, you'd be making me hurl it back up." Rico stuck out his tongue like he was trying to get a nasty taste out of his mouth.

My appetite had abandoned me. "I'm gonna go down to the lake and watch the sun set. C'mon, Chumley! We'll find you a dead animal to roll in." The dog rushed out of Jethro's tent, tripping on a rope and yanking a tent stake out of the ground.

"Hey," Jethro called after us. "Take my coffee pot with you and get me some more water, or you're gonna be the next dead animal he rolls in."

"Your threats don't scare me," I said, taking the coffee pot. "But if I fetch your water, I get some of your coffee."

"Fair enough. Don't lose my dog." Jethro knew that no matter how much trouble Chumley was, he more than paid for it in laughs. A little chaos is a small price to pay, because camping without a dog just wouldn't be the same.

That's right, Chumley.

Good Boy.

10

THE SKINNY DIP

MY FATHER-IN-LAW WAYNE IS ONE OF THE MOST PLEASANT, CARING AND thoughtful people I've ever met. He would never consider playing a prank on someone or deliberately trying to embarrass another human being. My brothers and I attribute this to the fact that he has three daughters and a wife, and so spent most of his adult life surrounded by non-male people with good manners, hygiene and tender sensibilities.

Whenever we invite him on one of our camping trips, it usually takes us at least two solid days to get him reprogrammed and acting normal again. It's a thankless task, but we don't mind. He'd do it for us. As long as his wife and daughters weren't around to shame him out of it.

One such trip was to a remote mountain lake in central Oregon, which my brother Jethro promised was only "a couple" of miles from the trailhead. I had followed my tried and true practice of packing enough supplies for myself and a small army of angry Cossacks, so my backpack weighed just slightly less than a 1972 Buick.

After we had hiked 'a couple of miles' a couple of times over, my kneecaps were threatening to take a permanent vacation from the rest of me. I collapsed onto a log next to the trail, not even bothering to take off my pack. My brother Rolf came over, looking concerned. I looked up, hoping that he might offer to carry some of my load. Then he whipped out a camera, snapped a picture of me, and walked off. So much for compassion. I lay my head back and groaned.

"What's your problem?" Jethro asked as I lay there in agony. "What are ya, a sissy?"

"Cork it," I gasped. "Your 'couple of miles' has turned into a couple of marathons, ya moron! If we don't see the lake by the time we cross the next rise, I'm gonna clonk you on the head with that walking stick and take away your beer. Then I'm gonna camp right next to the trail until some Granola comes by and rescues me. This blows!"

"Crybaby," Jethro said with a grin. "The lake's just around the corner. Trust me."

Trusting Jethro was low on my list of priorities. As it turned out, the lake was *not* just around the corner. The only thing that saved Jethro was that my kneecaps were still on strike and I couldn't catch up to kill him. We hiked another twenty minutes before finally getting to the lake, where we all collapsed in various states of exhaustion.

"Oh, what a beautiful setting!" Wayne exclaimed, beaming.

"Why did I bring all this crap?" I whined, rooting through my pack. I had extra clothes, rain gear, rope, three different skinning knives, various pots and pans, more stove fuel than I could possibly use in a month, and a six pack of beer.

Ooh, beer!

"Aren't you gonna set up your tent?" Jethro asked.

I eyeballed him over my upturned beer bottle. "Mm-mmm."

"Suit yourself," he said. He dug in his pack. "I'm gonna whip me up some mac and cheese."

I made a face, but finished my beer anyway. "Ahhhhhhh."

"Feeling better?" Wayne asked, giving me an affectionate pat on the shoulder.

"I'll feel better when Jethro burns his mac and cheese and Rolf falls in the lake."

Wayne looked slightly uncomfortable, glancing at Jethro and Rolf to see if their feelings were hurt. Jethro whistled happily. Rolf flashed an evil grin.

"Uhh, would you like some help setting up your tent?" Wayne asked me.

"Yeah, sure," I said. I wasn't really feeling ungrateful - I just wasn't ready to be quite so pleasant. He helped me set my tent up in a nice spot, then offered to share his dinner with me. I was starting to feel a bit more pleasant and thoughtful. Then Rico announced that he was going to hike around the lake. "Watch out for The Foot," I warned.

"Don't get lost," Jethro said.

"Don't listen to him," Rolf added. "Go ahead and get lost."

"Have a nice time!" Wayne said. We all stopped what we were doing and looked at him. He was probably going to need an emergency considerate-ectomy before the day was out.

Rico vanished into the trees, heading for the far side of the lake.

JETHRO MANAGED TO AVOID LIGHTING HIS MAC AND CHEESE ON FIRE AND Rolf refused to fall in the lake, so we were running low on entertainment. We settled for drinking our beers and bragging. Wayne listened politely, but didn't offer any boasts of his own. I was beginning to think his condition was critical when a distant shout drifted across the lake.

"Heyyyy, you guys!"

I looked across the lake, straining to see where the shout came from. I could see a vaguely human shape perched on a boulder at the far shore.

"Is that Rico?" Wayne asked.

I grabbed for my binoculars. "I think so..." I couldn't figure it out, but something about Rico's clothes didn't look right. They were all vaguely the same sickly hue of pink. I raised the binoculars just as he leaped into the air...

"COWABUNGA!!" he hollered... and suddenly snapped into terrifyingly clear focus as he pulled his legs to his chest in a perfect cannonball.

Completely naked.

"My eyes!" I shrieked, dropping the binoculars.

"Did he just jump in the lake naked?" Wayne asked, eyes slightly wide.

"That sounds about right," Rolf said. "You have to remember, he *is* a degenerate. Now where did I leave my camera?" He rummaged furiously through his pack, found the camera, and hustled off toward the far end of the lake.

"What's he doing with the camera?" Wayne asked me in a whisper.

"Exploring options for blackmail, I guess." I had already regained my eyesight and started on my second beer. Wayne looked worried.

SOME TIME LATER, ROLF WANDERED BACK INTO CAMP. "GET ANY GOOD shots?" I asked.

"He wouldn't hold still," Rolf said. "All I got was a few blurry pics that look like fake footage of The Foot without hair."

Wayne looked relieved.

Then Rico came back into camp, grinning. "Whoo! That water was coo-oold! Makes you feel alive!"

Jethro cracked open a beer. "You're a moron."

"Just 'cuz you've never *had* a bath doesn't mean it's too late to try," Rico said. "You could use it - you're gettin' a little gamey."

"And you're gettin' on my nerves, but that still won't make me jump in the lake nekkid. Pervert."

Rico smiled. "That's Mr. Clean, Refreshed Pervert to you."

We spent the rest of the afternoon trading insults and laughing at each other. Wayne laughed politely at some of the cracks, but mostly looked uncomfortable and worried about our feelings.

THE NEXT DAY, WE WOKE TO MORE OF THE SAME. WE SPENT THE MORNING hiking to another lake nearby, then retreated to our camp as the day warmed up. Rico dropped his day pack and headed for the far side of the lake again. Rolf waited a few seconds, then followed with his camera.

Several minutes later, we heard another "COWABUNGA" from across the lake. We didn't think much of it until a few minutes after that, when a young couple in their early twenties suddenly strolled right into our camp, carrying fishing poles.

"How's it going?" the young man asked, smiling.

"Great!" Wayne said, obviously relieved to have normal people to talk with. "How are you folks?"

"We're great!" the man said. "Just trying to catch some fish for dinner. You fellas do any fishing here?"

"No, we're just here to camp," Wayne said. "But help yourselves, there's plenty of room." I think Wayne expected them to fish right there near our camp - where Rico wouldn't be quite so obvious.

"Thanks!" the man said. "C'mon, hon - let's look for a spot on the other side of the lake so we don't bother these fellas."

Wayne's eyes got wide. Jethro and I stifled laughter. My oldest brother, Pike, grinned but kept quiet. "Good luck!" I called after them. They vanished into the trees in the same direction Rico and Rolf had gone.

"Boy, this is gonna be a hoot!" Jethro burst out laughing.

"I hope Rolf gets some good pictures!" I was giggling in anticipation.

Pike chuckled. "Rico should know better than that. Rolf never goes anywhere without that camera. Rico's gonna end up on the cover of Field and Scream!" Pike is by far the most polite and considerate of my brothers. But he still wouldn't let good manners get in the way of a laugh at Rico's expense.

Wayne looked nearly distraught. "Aren't you going to warn him?" he asked. "They'll SEE him!"

"Warn him?" I asked, looking over at Jethro. "What for?" We both cackled out loud.

Wayne looked from Jethro to me, to Pike, and back again. He was beside himself with anxiety. When none of us made any move to save Rico from humiliation, Wayne hurried off in pursuit of the young couple, hoping to preserve their innocence and Rico's dignity.

MEANWHILE, ACROSS THE LAKE, RICO HAD MANAGED TO FINISH HIS SWIM before hypothermia set in. He had dragged himself out onto a large flat rock, where he lay in the buff as the warm sun dried his pasty flesh. Rolf was thrashing around in the brush some distance away, trying to circle around to get ahead of Rico and catch him unawares. The young couple walked happily toward Rico's spot, chatting and laughing in blissful ignorance.

Rico heard them coming, but was too late to get dressed. He slid sideways off the large rock and wedged his body between two boulders, draping his jeans over his lower parts and hoping that the newcomers wouldn't notice he wasn't actually *in* his pants.

"Hi there!" the young man greeted Rico. "Having any luck?"

"Erm… no," Rico said, trying to be nonchalant. "I'm not fishing - just enjoying the sunshine. Heh, heh."

"Isn't it a beautiful day?" the young lady exclaimed, stepping closer. "I just love being in the wilderness on a sunny day, don't you?"

Go away, lady, Rico thought. *You're making small talk with a naked stranger who has a boulder poking him in the arse.* "Oh, yeah, I just love it," he said, shifting his weight and trying to keep the jeans from sliding off his lap.

The couple continued making small talk for several more minutes, oblivious to Rico's discomfort. Finally, as he lost all feeling in his legs, they turned to go. "Well, we better get going if we want to catch anything before dark," the man said. "Enjoy the sunshine!"

Rico waited until he was sure they were out of sight, then dragged himself from between the two rocks. His numb legs caused him some trouble getting his pants back on, which gave Rolf the opportunity to get better pictures. Back at camp, he threatened to email them to Rico's wife so she could see what a degenerate she married.

"She already knows," Rico said. "Your threats don't scare me."

Rolf was disappointed. "Well, maybe I'll just email them to all you guys, instead."

"Now who's the degenerate?" Jethro asked.

"I'll pass," Pike said, making a face.

"Ugh. Leave me out," I said. "I already nearly went blind seeing that slob in the buff from long distance. Close ups would probably kill me." I looked at my father-in-law. "Wayne, you interested?"

Wayne flinched. "What? Who, me? NO!! What is WRONG with you people?!?" We all looked at him. He seemed slightly annoyed, and appeared to be developing a facial tic. This was good, since angry resistance is one of the first steps toward recovery from terminal niceness.

LATER THAT AFTERNOON, JETHRO WAS FIDDLING AROUND WITH HIS CAMP stove, trying to heat water for coffee. As I was trying to think up a good insult, Wayne suddenly spoke up.

"You're not over fond of your eyebrows, are you, Jethro?"

"Shaddap, you…" he looked up. "Oh, it was you, Wayne. Sorry, I thought that sap MP was trying to insult me."

"He's not quick enough on his feet," Wayne quipped.

"Hey!" I protested. "What did I do?"

"Nothing," Wayne said. "That's what makes you such a good target." He was clearly warming to his craft at this point. Maybe a little too much. "Don't mind him, Jethro," he went on. "Just let me get my camera ready before you light your stove - I don't want to miss the fireball."

"Ooh! Good idea!" Rolf grabbed for his camera too.

As we hiked back to the trucks the next day, we passed another small lake, where another young couple was fishing. "Hey Rico," Wayne called out. "Ya feel like a swim?"

"No, thanks," Rico said. We all laughed. It seemed that Wayne was cured.

Our intervention, however, didn't stick. As soon as we pulled into Wayne's driveway, he instantly reverted to his former polite, considerate self. He told his wife how much he'd missed her; he fussed over his daughters; then he offered me a cool drink. Deep down inside, I silently lamented our failure. Then my mother-in-law asked if he got any good pictures. Wayne looked sideways at me.

"Some," he said. "But Rolf got some really good ones. I'll have him email them to you."

ABOUT THE AUTHOR

M.P. MacDougall is an American historian and author of thrillers, humorous satire and fantasy. The youngest of twelve children, he grew up on a suburban farm, spending much of his free time chasing cows, perfecting bicycle stunts and playing in the dirt, and he never had to wear a helmet or use anti-bacterial soap. He was a professional Air Traffic Controller for more than twenty-six years, and a practitioner of the art of sarcastic banter and snide commentary for much longer than that. He holds a Bachelor of Arts in World Military History, because he's afraid he'll lose it if he puts it down. He lives with his very patient wife and kids in the Pacific Northwest of the United States.

ALSO BY M.P. MACDOUGALL

Lawson Holland Thrillers

One Is A Warrior- FREE Novella download at MPMacDougall.com

The Blood of Tyrants

The Blood of Patriots

The Tree of Liberty

Sing Your Death Song

How To Steer Your Kid Series (Humor/Satire)

Jet Screamer

Meat Sandwiches

Harvey Bennett Prequels (With Nick Thacker)

The Icarus Effect

Learn more about the author at MPMacDougall.com

Thanks so much for reading!